"I bet you've always been the rebel type."

Caroline tilted her head to study him. Smiled.

"Exactly," he agreed. "Rebel. Ready to do outrageous deeds as long as they're for the love of a beautiful woman." He reached out and touched her cheek; his thumb outlined her full bottom lip. He ached to kiss her, but refused his own demands. "Have dinner with me tomorrow night."

"I can't. I have a business meeting."

"Cancel it. They're a dime a dozen. Say yes. Eight o'clock." He demanded it with every ounce of his being.

"We won't wind up like we did the last time, Tony. Never. It was a mistake. One I will never make again."

"You certainly know how to give a compliment." He smiled. "And *never* is such a long time."

Her answering smile lit his heart. "I think you might be the devil in disguise, Tony Valentine. You charm and wheedle your way into a woman's confidence, and then plead not guilty if anything happens."

Rita Clay Estrada, cofounder and first president of Romance Writers of America, didn't start out to be a writer. She studied art and psychology, worked as a model, a secretary, a salesperson and a bookstore manager. But Rita's countless fans are glad she found her true calling creating enthralling romances. *One More Time* is her twelfth romance for Harlequin Temptation. This talented author makes her home in Texas.

Books by Rita Clay Estrada

HARLEQUIN TEMPTATION

ONE MORE TIME

RITA CLAY ESTRADA

Harlequin Books

TORONTO • NEW YORK • LONDON
AMSTERDAM • PARIS • SYDNEY • HAMBURG
STOCKHOLM • ATHENS • TOKYO • MILAN
MADRID • WARSAW • BUDAPEST • AUCKLAND

Published July 1993

ISBN 0-373-25550-0

ONE MORE TIME

1

"BROTHER, DEAR, I *am* sitting down, even if it's on a hotel bed," Carolyn explained patiently as she fiddled with the telephone cord. She had just arrived in Corpus Christi and the sales meeting was in the morning. That meant there were hours of work to do tonight....

She heard Ed take a deep breath, then he blurted out his news. "Mike and Cora were killed in an auto accident this afternoon."

"Mike?" she repeated stupidly. "Cora?"

Ed began talking fast. "Look, I know you, Carolyn. You've been angry with them for four years, but you still care. That's why I'm calling instead of Mom. She's got enough to deal with right now. She can hardly speak without breaking off and staring into space. I doubt if she could keep it together if she had to tell you, too. She couldn't stand to hear you cry."

"Mother is always distant. So is Dad. You know that," Carolyn said coldly. "I learned from the same tutor you did, Ed. I don't cry. You know that."

"You should. And she's got a right to," Ed said soothingly. "She's barely coping with the death of her baby daughter."

Carolyn didn't hear any of it. Mother wasn't the focus of the problem. "This is a cruel joke. Right? Something you thought up to get me to acknowledge my feelings for my man-stealing sister and my own ex-husband." It was a script she knew, and it kept her from thinking about what Ed was really saying.

"Don't be a sore loser, Carolyn," Ed answered. "I was afraid you'd be like this. That's why I want you to rant and rave at me. Anything. But do something besides pretend it didn't happen."

Carolyn's heart still raced in denial. "Why are you doing this? It isn't funny, Edward. Not even your sense of humor could be this macabre."

"Dammit, Carolyn! Listen to me!" her brother exploded. "Mike and Cora are dead!"

The cold feeling she'd fought since first hearing her brother's voice on the hotel phone now invaded her very being.

"No!" she shouted, denying the feeling as well as the news.

"No," she repeated in a softer voice; now she was not denying his words but her own response.

"No. Please, dear God," she whispered. "No."

Ed's voice sounded tired. "Carolyn, if there's anything I can do." He paused. "I don't know what to say, dammit. I told Mom you'd rather hear it from me, but I just don't know."

"You did right, Ed," she said quietly after a moment.

"Damn!" her brother muttered. "I wish there was an easier way to do this. I wish you were here and I could help."

"It's all right, Ed," she said, functioning on automatic pilot. She had always reassured him. At one time that had been her job. To be strong...reassuring... giving to the family. And she had finally given everything she had, including her husband.

"I know it's a shock. But you're strong. You'll do okay, Carolyn."

She wondered whom he was reassuring—her or himself?

Absently she noticed she was welcoming that chilling feeling. It numbed her nerves and froze her emotions into a holding pattern. *Fine*, she told herself. *Everything will be fine.*

"Tell me what happened." She was sure her voice sounded as cold and distant as she felt.

"They were returning from Lake Conroe in that little Datsun 300Z of Cora's. The driver of a giant pickup was drunk and weaving down Interstate 45. He crossed the median and hit them head-on. They were killed immediately." Ed paused a moment. "Even the baby."

"Baby?"

Ed's sigh was heavy. "Ed?" Carolyn pressed for more, like someone checking the pain of a toothache. She needed to know. "Ed?"

"Cora was pregnant," he admitted finally.

Still no pain. "How far along?"

"Almost seven months."

Frost settled in the pit of her stomach, invaded her own empty womb. She and Mike had often discussed having children. He had always wanted children, and so had she, but she had thought that a child should be born only when both would-be parents were responsible, ready to face the challenge of child rearing. In her opinion, Mike hadn't been ready to be a parent.

Ed's voice seemed to boom hollowly through the receiver. "It was a girl."

An unbearable pain shafted her heart for a second. Then, with each shallow breath, the icy feeling spread to her very core until it, too, was frozen. "I didn't ask."

"You wanted to know." Ed was right. Bless him, he knew her well.

Carolyn forced herself to take another breath, then another. The cold had taken over her body, neutralizing the agony that she was sure lay just behind the next thought. She turned away from the misery. This wasn't the time. Later . . . later . . . later.

"I'll come home right away," she promised.

"Stay where you are for tonight, Carolyn, and wait until the morning to drive," Ed warned. "I don't think I could handle it if something happened to you, too."

"I'll be careful."

"No, wait until morning. It's already late. Please."

Carolyn glanced at the hotel alarm clock. It was almost ten. Ed was right. It was too late, and she was in no shape to drive for five hours on the highway. "I'll be at Mom's first thing in the morning," she assured her brother.

"I know. I'll meet you there." Ed's voice was stronger now, and she was grateful he was the one who had told her. "And, Carolyn—I might not say it often enough, but I love you, little sister."

Her fingers tightened around the receiver. "Thanks. I love you, too, big brother."

His voice was shaky when he answered. "You'd better. We're all we've got."

"We're enough," she answered. "We'll do just fine."

She held on to the phone long after the line went dead and replayed her brother's words. He loved her. Ed had never been one for saying sweet, mushy things to his two sisters, but he'd always shown in a hundred different ways just how much he loved them.

Growing up in an atmosphere that was an ugly blend of criticism and fear had given Carolyn, Ed and Cora a closeness that other siblings might not have had. No one else could understand how much a parent's withdrawal hurt, leaving bruises and wounds that no one could see.

They had suffered a different kind of abuse. Carolyn's mother and father had never beaten her—physically. But the constant criticism, the lack of touching or praise had taken their toll. From the time she could first remember, they'd feared the man who walked in every night and screamed abuse at everyone and everything in sight. Their mother had been afraid to show love to any of her children for fear of having him turn on the object of her affection. As Carolyn had grown older, she'd seen that her mom carried an equal share of the blame, for she'd refused to leave and had refused to fight. It was as if the family had lived under a black umbrella that shielded them from all the sunshine.

Until she'd left home and found Mike, she hadn't known someone could love and show it by praise and hugs and kisses....

Mike! She pushed that thought resolutely aside. It would kill her to think of him. Of Cora.

Carolyn stood and paced. Right now she had to keep all feeling at bay. Later, when she was home, she could break down. But not now, not here.

Grabbing her key, she walked out of the room. This was no time to be alone. As she punched the elevator button, she heard music drifting up from the bar. She glanced over the railing that ran around the atrium lobby and saw a few of the sales reps still checking in to this upper-grade, businessmen's hotel, catering to those who traveled for a living. That meant the food would be good and the bar full.

She headed for the bar.

After all, she had the rest of her life to think about her beloved Mike and Cora. And their baby. The rest of her nightmares....

TONY VALENTINE SAT at the end of the bar and wondered what the hell he was doing in Corpus Christi in the middle of summer. He was unlike most of the tourists flocking to Padre Island and its spun-sugar, sandy beaches. His trip was strictly business. Or, more precisely, the process of selling his business was what had brought him here.

He scanned the room, seeing faces he could see in any upscale hotel on a weekday. With a sense of relief, he realized that after negotiating the sales contract, he'd never have to be in one of these large, impersonal buildings again. He was sick of traveling, of dealing, of worrying about what the next salesman might be offering. He was tired of constantly running hard and fast, just to keep up with the Joneses, when he didn't even know them!

It was time to slow down. Selling his business was just the beginning. Next he'd sell the house he was supposed to call home. After that he'd lie back and smell the flowers for a while, then find something he wanted to do for the pure fun of it. If he could make a decent living while still enjoying life, he'd be happy. Since he would have enough money to last a lifetime, acquiring more wasn't the object of the game anymore. Personal happiness was the new goal. It had taken him a long time to get to this point, but now he'd made up his mind, he didn't think he'd regret it.

Life didn't give anyone second chances. And he'd lost too much not to appreciate what he had left. From now on he meant to enjoy it.

The bar doors swung open and Tony's attention was caught by a striking woman who stood just inside the entrance, probably waiting for her eyes to adjust to the dimness. He recognized her instantly. She had checked in about an hour ago, and he'd been right behind her in the line. At the time he'd thought he'd been hit by a thunderbolt, but there'd been no way to introduce himself. He'd hoped for a moment like this, and God had just handed it to him.

Shiny blond hair barely brushed her expensively suited shoulders. Her tobacco-brown shoes had spike heels, but on her they looked great. Her well-manicured hands clutched a purse that matched her shoes. She looked nervous, almost scared, yet full of bravado. He couldn't see the color of her eyes from where he sat, but locked his own on her, silently willing her to walk in his direction.

She seemed not to see him, but walked unerringly to the bar and sat down; only one stool separated them. She closed her eyes for a moment, then opened them again and stared at the bartender. Her eyes were as brown as those of a fallen doe.

"Gin and tonic with a twist." Her voice was low and soft; it touched him somewhere deep inside. He was shocked by his response.

The bartender nodded and began mixing. A moment later he placed the drink in front of her, then went to talk to a cocktail waitress at the other end of the mahogany bar.

Tony waited for the newcomer to look up, smile, and say something to him. Most women didn't sit this close to a man unless the bar was crowded or they were planning to strike up a conversation.

He studied her expression, struck by the incredible sadness that lurked in the shadows of those big, brown eyes. Why was such a beautiful woman so sad? He would have asked her, but it was a long time since he'd picked up a woman in a bar, and the idea of doing so now was distasteful.

Downing the last of his Amstel Light, he motioned to the bartender for another. A slow, old favorite tune began to play, but Tony hardly noticed. Now he was frustrated, aiming his anger at the blonde. He'd be damned if he'd acknowledge her. She could melt in the noonday, Corpus Christi sun before he'd . . .

"Would you care to dance?" Her voice was as soft and low as when she'd ordered her drink.

He looked up and stared straight into those soft, vulnerable eyes. "Are you talking to me?"

She nodded.

Tony smiled and stood, waiting for her to slip off the stool. When she did so, he took her hand—it was oddly chilly—and led her to the dance floor.

One hand rested on his shoulder, the other lay limply in his. Tony felt as if she were looking over his shoulder, seeing something other than the darkened recesses of the bar—something like another lifetime? Securing his hold on her waist, Tony brought her closer, wondering if she even realized she was being held.

Uttering a sigh that whispered warmly against his neck, she let her forehead drift to his shoulder. His grip tightened. He had no idea what was going on inside her head, but she clearly needed something, and he wanted to give it, whatever it was.

Her lightly sensual perfume filled his senses, and her cool hand began to take on the warmth of his own body heat. Her feet effortlessly found the same rhythm as his and they glided across the floor as if they were Fred Astaire and Ginger Rogers. But Tony was sure Ginger had never been held this close or felt this good.

The stranger caught her breath, and he knew she was steeped in some sadness. The memory of how he'd felt when his wife died rose unbidden. That overwhelming loneliness still caught him occasionally, at odd times. Although it had happened many years ago, he could still recognize the feeling. Could she have gone through something similar? He prayed not. He knew he was a very strong person, but remembered when he'd thought he wouldn't make it.

Tony pulled back. "Are you all right?"

Eyes still closed, she nodded. "Fine."

That dance ended, but Tony continued to hold the woman in his arms, swaying back and forth. The disc jockey was apparently smart enough to realize they were the only ones on the floor, so they might as well be catered to. The next selection was equally slow and danceable. Since she didn't protest, he assumed it was what she wanted, too.

Once around the floor, he nodded to the deejay to continue playing slow tunes. He didn't think there would be a problem, since there were only a few people scattered around the bar. It was, in fact, almost empty, except for a few businessmen in one corner.

Two dances blended into two more, then another two. With each succeeding dance, the woman in his arms snuggled closer until they were barely shuffling their feet to the beat. Her fingers, now warm, touched his neck and tickled his hair. That wasn't all she was tickling, but he had the good sense to keep himself in check.

She snuggled closer.

Tony had to muffle his groan.

The song ended. He took her back to her seat and ordered drinks for them both. She stared at the melting ice.

He had to know. "What's going on?"

She looked up, visibly confused. "What?"

Her thoughts were a thousand miles away. He would have to treat her more gently than he'd thought. "What's going on here?" he repeated. "You've asked me to dance, but we've never even exchanged names."

Tony thought he'd never seen a more beautiful smile. She stuck out her hand. "My name is Carolyn."

He took her hand and clasped it in his. "I'm Tony."

She smiled again.

"You're beautiful, Carolyn."

Her laugh ran down his spine in anticipation of . . . Of what? "You're very kind."

"Yes, I am."

"And very sure of yourself."

"Yes, I am," he repeated with a grin. "And slightly outrageous."

"I believe you," she answered, a delightful smile brushing her lips. "What do you do, Tony?"

So they were going to play bar games. He was disappointed until he realized that she had almost forgotten where they were. Those dances had told him more about her than she would like him to know. "I'm here to sell a company I own."

Her brows rose. "In what field?"

"Triage Marketing Research. It's twelve years old today, and I'm ready to bail out and relax for a while."

Carolyn's eyes widened appreciably. "I've heard of your company. It's good."

"Thanks. What have you heard about my company?"

"Just that it's the place to go for information. You canvass the entire country, like The Gallup Poll."

"You must be in a people-oriented business," he stated dryly; high-pressured jobs like his took a toll on people who enjoyed them, let alone those who didn't.

"No more than the next one," she said, accepting her new drink from the bartender. "But your company is at the top of its field. Don't you enjoy it?"

He shook his head. "That's why I'm selling. It's hard work to stay on top."

Taking a sip of her drink, Carolyn contemplated his words. She couldn't ever imagine giving up. "But I imagine that would be part of the challenge."

"It was in the beginning. But, like most things, it turned into drudgery. A lot like housework," he added with a smile. "You do the same job over and over until it's boring as hell."

Shaking her head in wonder, she said, "I've *never* found business boring."

"Not even when it interferes with fun?"

"Business *is* my fun," she told him with such sincerity that he had no choice but to believe her.

"How sad," he murmured.

"Not really. You can lose yourself in business, but fun is usually a scheduled thing."

"Even if you believe in reincarnation, this is the only life you'll remember. You might as well enjoy it."

She pushed a silken strand of blond hair behind one ear. He could see her considering his ideas and wondered why such a woman as beautiful as Carolyn would take pleasure in hiding from life behind her career. What was she afraid of?

"I did enjoy it," she retorted, staring into her drink as if answers were going to pop up from the bottom of the glass. "I do enjoy it."

The music began again. Carolyn looked so sad that Tony wanted to comfort her once more, though warning bells were going off in his head. He told himself that a workaholic was his worst choice for a dance partner. "Carolyn." It took her a moment to refocus her attention. When she did, he continued. "Dance with me again," he ordered gruffly and stood up.

Carolyn took one sip of her drink, then rose and obediently placed her hand in his. He walked her to the center of the dance floor and took her into his arms.

She seemed to have a split personality. A career woman who docilely followed directions—from a male, no less. A feminine woman, whose career seemed to demand all her free time. Which was the real Carolyn?

Once more she rested her head against his shoulder and her warm breath caressed his neck. His heart raced in reaction. He tightened his grip and pulled her closer, a low groan rising in his throat.

She made a soft, kittenish sound in return. He felt his blood thicken and pool in his legs.

Carolyn's hands lightly stroked the back of his head and neck, and heat immediately seared his spine, spreading through the rest of his body.

Tony brushed a kiss upon her temple and she burrowed her head deeper into his shoulder. He placed her other hand upon his shoulder and held her hips with both arms. The music shifted easily from one slow song to another, but he hardly heard a note.

Every nerve in his body was attuned toward Carolyn's tiniest movement, her every breath. They fitted so perfectly together that they could have been two pieces of a jigsaw puzzle. She tightened her arms around his neck. "Don't leave me."

He could have sworn tears fogged her voice. Pulling back, he looked into her face. Her eyes were closed, her lips slightly parted, showing the tips of white teeth.

Heart racing, he bent his head and placed a chaste kiss upon her mouth. "Are you sure?"

She nodded her head slowly. "Yes."

His groin tensed in anticipation, but his mind told him that tonight wasn't the right time. He would take her to her room and let her sleep off whatever had gone wrong. Tomorrow he'd take her to breakfast and get to know her better. Tomorrow...

"Let's go," he told her softly, forcing her to look up.

Luminous, brown eyes stared at him as if she'd never seen him before. For just a moment he saw pain so intense that it glazed her eyes and made her open her mouth in a silent "Oh." Then it was gone and she was staring at ... him.

Without looking back, she turned and headed for the lobby and the elevator. Tony was right behind her, watching her bottom sway enticingly from side to side. Feminine. Very feminine.

They stepped into the elevator and she pushed the floor button. He couldn't stand it anymore. It didn't matter that he would leave her at the door of her room. Right now he needed to touch her.

Reaching for her hand, he took it into his own. That must have startled her. Eyes darted up to look at him, then quickly back to the elevator panel.

Tony refused to let go. "Don't worry," he said softly. "I'm walking you to your room. That's all."

Carolyn didn't answer.

The elevator stopped and they stepped off. She turned, leading him, fingers still entwined with his, down the hall to her room. Reaching into her skirt pocket, she pulled out a key and handed it to him.

Tony reluctantly let go her hand and fitted the key into the lock. It didn't matter what his body craved; he was going to leave well enough alone. He pushed the door open and held out the key.

Suddenly it was as if Carolyn had awakened from a dream. She stared at the key, then at him. She smiled slowly, and covered his hand with her own. A light tugging motion brought him into her room.

The bathroom light was on and the door partly closed, so it was just bright enough for him to see where the furniture was. She stopped and faced him at the foot of the bed.

"Carolyn . . ." he began, but she shook her head.

Her arms curled around his neck as she pulled his mouth down to her own. She leaned into him, allowing him to feel her soft curves against his own taut body. Warmth spiraled to his toes. Her kiss was firm and strong and demanded an answer; it was something he wanted to give more than anything he'd ever wanted before. Her tongue softly dueled, then melded with his, hinting at how they would play if they made love— *when* they made love.

He pulled back to tell her no, but she tightened her hold just enough to show her protest. "Don't leave," she whispered, breathing into his mouth. "Please."

Again he heard that sad catch in her throat.

He wanted to tell her that he *had* to leave now. He couldn't continue like this without making mad, passionate love with her. His hands moved over her arms, then cupped her throat and neck. Logical thought died. "I'm not going anywhere. I promise."

She must have understood his need. Her hands sought his tie and slipped it out of its knot. Then she reached for the buttons of his dress shirt, undoing them one by one.

Tony stood completely still, searching her face. Was this crazy? Was this a dream? This was his personal, number one fantasy. He was watching a woman he badly wanted undress him.

His hand covered hers, halting her movements. Her eyes gazed up at him, large and questioning. "Why?" he asked.

She didn't look away this time, and he saw the pain reappear. Once more tears filmed her eyes, making them seem luminescent in the dimness. "Because I need to be held and touched. Because I need to feel loved. Just for tonight." Her voice dropped to a whisper. "Don't let me be alone. Not yet."

Tony's hands shook as he undid the rest of his shirt and pulled it out of his waistband. Then he slipped off his shoes. Chest bare, he stood in front of her. "Lady, I can't imagine anything I'm more willing to do than be with you."

Relief lightened her eyes. Holding his eyes with her own, she dropped her suit jacket to the floor, then slowly undid her blouse and skirt and let them follow.

Standing in a black silk teddy that set his heart racing erratically, she tilted her head. Blond hair spilled over one shoulder and casually hid a strap.

She stared at him, clearly appraising him. "Are you going to remain dressed?" Her voice was low and teasing, her gaze openly sensuous.

"Are you?" he shot back, hearing his own voice husky with desire.

In answer she gave a low, soft chuckle.

With the artistry of a striptease, Carolyn shrugged one shoulder and let a thin, black strap fall to her arm. A finger pushed the other one down. The teddy slipped smoothly to the floor. Thigh-high hose stayed up without benefit of a garter belt, and he watched as she peeled them off and carelessly tossed them aside. She had the most unbelievably pale, soft skin he'd ever seen.

They stared at each other for a long moment. Tony's breath wheezed in his throat. Her small, pointed breasts moved slightly with each shallow breath she took. Her gaze dropped to his waist, then caught his again. He got the message.

Tony undid his belt and took off his pants and socks. For a moment he stared at her, wondering at the whim of the gods. Why did he deserve such a rich reward? She was so breathtakingly lovely, he couldn't swallow.

He reached for her waist, clasping it in a steady grip but bringing her no closer. "You're beautiful, but you probably already know that."

"I'm no different from anyone else. I need to hear it. Thank you." Her voice was a whisper that aroused him even more. She took a step forward and rested her forehead against his lightly haired chest. Without her heels she barely came to the top of his shoulder.

Her sigh shivered down his already taut body, and he was torn between throwing her onto the bed and making love, or putting his arms around her to protect and comfort her from whatever demons were chasing her. After a second's hesitation, he drew her close and held her.

Carolyn stiffened a little, then relaxed. She had chosen to trust him. Now he hoped he could live up to that trust, if only for tonight.

He stroked the silken strands of her hair and the back of her neck. Her skin felt soft, her hair like spun sugar under his slightly callused palm. "Tell me about it."

Hurt darkened her eyes, then she shook her head. "Not now. Later. Maybe."

"Are you sure?"

She nodded, and her warm breath fanned his abdomen again. Her arms came around his waist and cradled the small of his back. The light from her bathroom bathed the hall, but didn't reach the bedroom. The downtown lights barely penetrated the heavy drapes, but he could just see her smaller, pale outline against his own, darker one. Ivory skin glistened under his hands. With every beat of his heart, his need grew stronger.

The one word he uttered came from his throat as a strangled cry. "Carolyn..."

Lifting her head from his chest, she looked up. Then she cupped his face in her hands. "Shh, it's all right. I promise. It's all right." Her voice was a husky whisper.

Her lips brushed his, pulling away before he could deepen the embrace into the kiss he wanted so badly.

Tony sought the softness of her breasts. He rubbed his thumbs over the nipples, feeling them react instantly to his touch. She drew in a sharp breath. Her eyes closed, and he felt tension build in her. He did it again and again and knew she was as sensitive there as she would be elsewhere. Her responses were immediate, and that was as much of an aphrodisiac as watching her.

She was all pliable flesh, moving toward him, with him, as he shifted his hands. With every stroke, a light, shimmering tremor passed through her; again she opened her eyes to stare at him.

"That feels so good."

"That's just the beginning," he replied hoarsely, needing to taste the firmness of her breasts, to run his tongue around the pebble-hard nipples. Just thinking about it was driving him crazy.

Then, with all the confidence of a woman of the world, all the innocence of a girl child who has never known an adult man's true hunger, Carolyn led him to the king-size bed that dominated the room.

He knew what to do from there.

2

CAROLYN BLOCKED OUT the pain that was waiting to overwhelm her. The time to deal with death would come soon enough. Right now, desire proved that she was alive.

She was thankful Tony was here. He'd help keep the nightmares at bay. Tony, with his thick, overlong hair that felt like satin threads, blue-gray eyes she could melt into, and a touch that set fires throughout her body. Handsome and strong, Tony made her feel like celebrating the never-ending dance of life instead of analyzing its tragic end. Tony would keep the chill away and warm her.

The mattress gave way as he lay down beside her and flesh brushed flesh. His chest touched her breasts, legs intertwined with softer limbs, stomachs met. Her thoughts fled. His attraction to her was, she thought, more obvious than hers to him, but no stronger. She took pleasure in the fact that he couldn't hide his need for her; it gave her a feeling of being in control. Someone handsome and sensitive had responded and wanted her. Not to her sister, but to *her*. Someone big and strong and sweet and kind.

Tony's every gesture, every touch was gentle and brought healing. He read her moves, anticipated her thoughts before they became wants. He forced her to think only of him, and that was exactly what she needed.

His dark head was bent over her breast, teasing a taut, dusky nipple. Strong, lightly callused hands searched for other, still more tender, pleasure points. Her breath caught in her throat; his touch was wonderful, tempting, and was sending her wild. Passion was building like a carefully tended flame, growing into a fire out of control. Her muscles contracted at his every touch until her head whirled, dizzy with wonder.

Her own hands weren't idle. She let them explore his strong, masculine flesh. He was lean and sinewy, leashed strength that found plenty of ways to let her know who was leading this dance, but she knew her own movements were equally telling.

"Touch me more." His voice was hoarse with need.

"Where?" she asked, hearing her own voice wispy and breathless. "Here? Here? Or here?" Her fingers teasingly played over his flesh.

His breathing stopped. Then a low chuckle echoed through the quiet. "Dear, sweet heaven," he muttered. "All of the above."

She smiled and continued to tease him with the light, skimming touch of her manicured nails. "What about here? And here? Does your back have any sensitive spots? What nice buns! Are they sensitive, too? And your thighs? They're like strong tree trunks. Do they like to be touched?"

She outlined his collarbone with her tongue, tasting the clean saltiness. "And here?" she asked again, aware of her own audacity. "What about here?"

He uttered a low groan and let his mouth capture hers, putting an end to her words of torture, if not to her touch. His lips were firm and hot and moist, his tongue dueling sensuously for domination. Carolyn answered back in kind, unwilling to let him win. Their battle ended when the kiss did.

Once more he bent his head and teased a nipple with his tongue. But when he took her soft flesh into his mouth, she thought she'd die from the exquisite pleasure.

"Tony," she whispered, shifting her legs. "Please, Tony. Now."

"Not yet," he murmured. "Wait, sweet. Wait."

Her arms encircled his waist, pulling him closer. But not close enough. Desire and passion escalated; now their name was need, burning like a furnace, deep inside her. She wanted him. *Now.*

Still he refused.

His warm mouth traveled from one breast to the other, teasing each nipple into taut attention. Strong hands skimmed over her ribs and stomach to reach the soft tendrils that hid her desire. She moaned with wonder at his intimate touch. When his finger slipped inside to the source, she thought she couldn't take any more.

"Please," she begged again.

"No. Not yet," he answered.

Both possessive and kind, he claimed her lips, leading her through a labyrinth of sensations that were foreign to her. Her hands learned the hard contours of his body.

She heard a light, kittenish sound and vaguely realized it was her own. Opening her eyes, she cupped his face with her hands and looked up. His eyes were so blue, they were almost black. His expression was tense.

"Tony..."

His answer was a groan that let her know just how much restraint he was using. It satisfied her sense of fair play; she wasn't the only one suffering from this particular brand of torture.

He turned away briefly, she heard a rustling sound, then he finally raised himself over her; she sighed. Soon the anguish of anticipation would be exchanged for a feeling of total completion.

Clamping his mouth upon hers in a gesture of complete possession, Tony entered her. She moaned his name, letting her hands stray over his hips and back as she pressed him to her. Almost immediately, stars and brilliant colors burst through her mind, her body, sending her spiraling ever higher. Tony's body responded the same way, and their voices mingled in the warm breath between them. . . .

"Am I still alive?" he murmured in her ear several minutes later. She laughed lightly, encircling his lean back with her arms.

"You certainly are," she stated firmly, underlining their closeness.

The hands that had earlier sought secret pleasure now soothed fevered flesh. Kisses that had been urgent were now slow and light and tender.

Carolyn loved the feeling of Tony's weight. It was warm, comforting and...connecting. As long as he was here, she was not alone.

She tightened her hold on his waist. "Don't go," she begged. "Don't leave me alone." As long as Tony was with her, she could keep the terrible thoughts locked up. Tony kept the loneliness away.

"I won't." He nuzzled her neck, then sought the soft underside of one ear. "Promise."

Assured that he would do as she asked, Carolyn relaxed. Tony curled her possessively into the curve of his body and she slept.

Sometime in the night they separated. Later, Tony heard her whimper. He drew her closer, lightly caressing her side and hip with one hand. His mouth brushed her temple, then moved down to her shoulder. "Shh, it's all right."

She gave another little cry and he repeated his words. She must have heard his reassurance, because she soon grew calm. Strangely, so did he.

Several hours later she was awakened by more of Tony's caresses. His mouth nuzzled her shoulder, his fingers sought her sweet, private places. She turned toward him willingly and they made love once more, exploring each other without the frenetic activity of the first time.

Then, as morning light edged its way through the curtains, Carolyn reached for Tony and touched him, silently asking to make love with her again. This time it was the slow and leisurely lovemaking that comes after sleep and comfort and satiation. Wonderful.

A short time later, Tony looked at the bedside clock and realized he had to be at his meeting in less than an hour. Not wanting to wake her, he carefully eased himself away. He glanced over his shoulder to make sure she was still asleep, then couldn't resist the urge to pull up the sheet to cover her bared shoulder. Naked, he slipped off the bed and walked to the bathroom. A few minutes later he was dressed.

Tony leaned over and gently brushed a kiss upon Carolyn's brow. In sleep she was even more beautiful. Her hair, so well combed last night, was thoroughly tousled now. Her skin seemed to glow. Carolyn looked like a woman who had savored being loved, and that pleased him above all things. She smiled in her sleep, snuggled deeper into the sheets, then frowned.

Later he'd have to discover what it was that made her so unhappy that she cried in her sleep. Now he was late for his meeting. Quickly he scribbled a few words on the back of his business card and laid it upon the dresser. It was only a security measure. He'd be back within the next half hour. To make sure of that, he took her key from its spot on top of the TV, so that he could get in again after cleaning up for his meeting.

As he opened the door, he glanced down and saw on the floor the quick-exit pass the hotel gave to preferred customers. Boldly printed on the front of the envelope in black ink was Carolyn's last name: Perkins.

Smiling and taking a last look over his shoulder, he closed the door behind him and headed down the hall. He'd clean up and dress in his own room, then come by to wake Carolyn before she left. Now that he'd found her, he wanted to romance her—to take her to dinner and learn everything about her, the way he should have done last night. This was the beginning of something very special. He wasn't going to let her go.

He couldn't wait to have done with the negotiations. Once everything was settled and taken care of, he'd have all the time in the world to pursue Carolyn Perkins.

AT THE SOUND of the door shutting Carolyn sat up in bed and swung her feet to the floor. She breathed a sigh of relief. She had wanted him to be gone by the time she awoke. Truth was, she didn't want to admit she might have been waiting for him to leave before she could wake up completely and face what she had done.

Memories of her aggressive behaviour last night swam through her head, making her flush in embarrassment. She had been so different. Brazen. Elemental. Earthy.

She groaned aloud and placed her head in her hands. Why hadn't she driven home last night?

How could she have done such a thing? She'd actually *dragged* a man upstairs and made love to him; not once, not twice, but three times!

If she was right, Tony would probably return to her room before noon. He might be back after his meeting was over, but she had a feeling he would be here sooner than later. She needed to get out of here. Pronto.

A glance at the top of the TV confirmed that her room key was missing. Her hunch about the man was right. Tony wasn't going to fade into the woodwork and allow her to disappear from his life. He wasn't about to let her call the shots, especially when the call she had in mind was to pretend they didn't know each other.

She had a feeling that he wasn't the type for a one-night stand. She'd never been one, either. Until now. Had she given him more than just her first name? She didn't think so. All the same, the only way she'd be sure not to see Tony again would be if he couldn't find her. That left her only one recourse.

Moving quickly, Carolyn grabbed underwear from the suitcase on the chair, aimed for the bathroom and flipped on the water for the shower. Within five minutes she was applying makeup and slipping into a dress. Fifteen minutes later, she was ready to go. She signed the hotel's quick-exit option and placed it carefully on top of the TV set. It was a little after seven-thirty. She called the front desk and told them she was leaving. The bill would be charged to her credit card.

Aware that the blush of satisfying lovemaking still stained her cheeks, she prayed she would never be in this hotel—or see Tony—again. Just thinking about her wanton behavior embarrassed her again.

Striding out the hotel doors into the warm morning air, she promised herself that she would forget last night. For good.

Right now she had enough to cope with. Her parents needed her help. Curious bystanders would be watching for her reaction to this tragedy. She'd been the target of such speculation once. She didn't need that again.

Having her wits about her meant not thinking about a night spent with a man whose last name she didn't know and whose handsome face she didn't want to remember.

It was time to go home for a funeral.

SMILING, Tony stepped off the elevator and opened Carolyn's door. The drapes were still drawn, so the room was dim. He walked to the bed, his eyes adjusting as he went.

She was gone.

He glanced toward the bathroom, remembering that the door had been open, the room dark. He felt a pain in his chest.

He flipped on the side light and looked around. One glance confirmed what he already knew. She'd left as quickly as she could. Even her suitcase had to have been packed in haste, for several hotel hangers lay on the floor by the chair. In front of the TV, he saw a small, glittering object. He bent and picked it up. It was her earring, a stud diamond, expensive and tasteful.

His card was still sitting on the dresser. She had either chosen not to take it with her or hadn't even seen it. Because of the angle at which it lay, he would guess the latter. She obviously hadn't taken the time for a last look around, or she would have wondered what the scrap of white paper was.

Pulling out his monogrammed handkerchief, Tony wrapped the earring in it, put it into his jacket pocket and walked out of the room. Cold determination took over.

Carolyn might have thought she'd seen the last of him, but she was wrong. She might not remember him—after all, she didn't know his last name—but he would remember her. *He* knew hers.

Tony went to his own room and dialed the front desk. "This is Room 346. Do I have any messages?" He listened to the answer he was expecting. There were none.

"When did my associate, Carolyn Perkins, check out?"

"Sometime around seven thirty-five this morning."

"Thank you." He hung up the phone very quietly. Taking a deep breath, he forced himself to release it slowly, but inside his emotions were bubbling like a volcano.

She'd left the hotel over ten minutes ago, within twenty minutes of his leaving her room. That meant she must have awakened immediately after he left.

Unless she'd been feigning sleep.

Tony felt his gut clench. Was she so afraid of him? Did he frighten her? Was that why she'd whimpered in her sleep?

"No," he declared grimly to the empty room.

Even though he knew he shouldn't, he felt betrayed by what she'd done. Damn her! How could she make love with him and then walk away, as if it had meant nothing? He was a damn sight more than just a provider of an amusement. But she didn't know that. In fact, she'd picked him up, then thrown him away, just as easily. God, it was a horrible feeling! He felt more like a thing than a human being.

He wanted to laugh at his naive way of thinking. Wasn't that supposed to be how a woman felt when a guy set up a one-night stand and then disappeared? Yet here it was—the circumstances were reversed. He was the one left feeling hurt. But he did have the diamond earring.

He had to find her again, if for no other reason than to prove to her that she had missed a golden opportunity. He was worth more, much more, than she seemed to believe. He deserved better treatment.

Inside his briefcase was a check for a little over a million dollars, the first payment from the sale of his business. The rest would come in two more installments and some stock transfers over the next three months. That knowledge helped assuage the pain of his kicked and bruised ego.

He wanted to see her, talk to her and let her know that she had thrown away something of value. It was a crazy idea, he knew, but it was there, just the same. He wanted Carolyn to regret throwing him away, to find out what a catch he was, even if she wasn't interested in catching him.

His anger flared again. He didn't know how or when or where, but he'd find her, tell her off, then watch her crumble at the realization that she could have had heaven in her arms—every night.

Moving swiftly, economically, Tony packed his suitcase, conscious that he was being childish. He guessed that he'd probably beaten Carolyn's speed record in packing, but after all, anger was still driving him.

He'd find her. He'd find her and teach her a lesson in manners that she'd never forget. No one—man or woman—should be so callous with another human being's feelings. He refused to ask himself why he felt so hurt, and the fact that he couldn't put the matter aside made him even angrier, more frustrated.

Carolyn had inadvertently done him good, he thought, trying to find the up side to the situation, as he strode to the elevators. After giving every scrap of talent and energy for years to his work, he was now free to do whatever he wanted. He didn't know what the future held for him, but he knew what he was going to do first. He'd find Carolyn Perkins and show her what a mistake she had made.

CAROLYN SAT IN CHURCH, her brother on one side, her parents on the other. She stared at the coffins in front of her and wondered when feeling would return. So far there was nothing—no tears, no cries—not even a sense or remorse. That wonderful numbness was still with her, and she was thankful for it. Her family had enough to contend with right now, without rehashing old problems.

Looking back, she had to admit that all her life she'd tried too hard. She'd had to be the best, to make the best grades, to be head cheerleader, to be on the winning debating team.

Along with all that, she'd had to be mother and father and sister to her siblings. She'd found the answers to their questions, given them the comforting hugs, taken the occasional blows and always assumed the responsibility for whatever action had set off her father's tirades.

During her college days, her parents had seemed to ignore her, but still she'd had to go home, to tell them of her triumphs. Their lack of interest had driven her— she'd been willing to do anything to get their attention.

It had taken her a while to catch on to the destructive pattern. Once she had, she'd gone into counseling with a therapy group on campus. What she'd learned there about herself had proven invaluable. She had learned how to make herself emotionally independent of her parents, how to set goals for herself—and attain them.

She'd met Mike in her senior year in college. It had been love at first sight, and they'd married eight weeks later. Then she'd had her brother, sister and her husband as her family.

Four years ago, her newly reconstructed family had fallen apart. So had her world. Four years ago, her husband's infidelity with her sister had destroyed the family, and nothing had been the same since. No Thanksgivings together. No Christmas mornings of temporary peace and goodwill.

Carolyn had divorced Mike. And Cora had tried, over and over again, to explain how they just "couldn't help themselves" and to beg for forgiveness.

"How can we *not* be friends now, when we've been through so much together? How can you turn off your emotions so well? I know you've always been the strong one, Carolyn, but that's plain heartless!" her sister had cried, just two years ago after another failed attempt at reconciliation.

Carolyn hadn't been able to form the words to tell her sister that just thinking about Cora and Mike together hurt so much, she thought she'd die from the pain. How did one tell one's sister that she had stolen more than just a husband? That all of Carolyn's dreams and hopes and love had been taken away when Cora stole Mike. And if they had been as close as Carolyn had believed shouldn't her sister have known what immense pain it would cause?

Cora had not only stolen Carolyn's husband, but also Carolyn's relationship with her sister and the new family she had built. Cora had only lost her sister, but Carolyn had lost three people and a dream.

Now all she had left surrounded her. Here they sat: a family again, temporarily united by tragedy. Now it seemed as if she should have found the words for forgiveness. She should have . . . Her hands shook at the thought of all the wasted time, with the yearning to put things right. Too late, too late, too late. . . .

Ed took her hand into his and gave it a light squeeze of reassurance. She squeezed back, knowing he needed even more comfort than she did. Ed had always been caught in the middle between his two sisters. He probably felt guilty at not forcing the issue of peace with Cora.

Face it, Carolyn, she told herself. *Even you subconsciously believed that the time would come when the*

three of us would make peace. No matter what, it
hadn't been all Cora's or Mike's fault.

Now it was too late.

Still she didn't cry.

For a fleeting, outrageous moment, she craved to be
back in bed with Tony, making mindless love with him,
then being held and comforted until she fell into a deep,
dreamless sleep.

She jolted herself back to the present. It was awful to
think of making love with one man when she was at the
funeral of another! She locked her gaze on Mike's cof-
fin. Why couldn't he occasionally have shown just a
little of the tenderness Tony had given her?

Once more she gave herself a mental shake. Tony had
been a fling. He was not like Mike, who'd been her
husband, friend and lover. Given time, she was sure
that Tony, too, would show feet of clay. Everyone did.
The trick was to keep those feet hidden.

Her parents, holding each other, still shutting out Ed
and herself, stood and filed out of the church. Everyone followed suit. Once the cemetery service was over,
she could go home and lock herself inside the privacy
of her own house. There no one would wonder why she
didn't—or couldn't—cry. She would be blessedly
alone, no one watching her or commenting on her behavior. No one would be able to call her brave, cou-
rageous, forgiving or—worst of all—strong.

She used to believe she was strong. But time had taught her that Cora was stronger. Cora, who'd pretended that she was weak and shy and unable to do a single thing on her own! Cora, who'd manipulated others into being and doing whatever it was that she wanted. Cora, who had duped everyone, including her big sister.

Carolyn was just plain stupid.

AFTER THE INTERNMENT she drove straight home, even though her brother and his sweet wife, Tammy, had begged her to come to their house for dinner. It was time to be alone to shed her public image.

Once inside, she unzipped her plain black dress and hung it on the doorknob of the master bedroom. She slipped off her black pumps and left them there, too. She walked into the kitchen in her black teddy and poured herself a glass of white wine.

Tony's words came back to her. "Tell me about it," he had said. She wished she'd been able to. She wished she could talk to someone who would listen to her. How could you put all that hurt and loneliness into one sentence? *My husband left me for my sister.* Her brother's loyalty was torn. Her parents would never discuss the matter, because their policy was to suppress any unpleasantness. She had no one to turn to. Soupy though it sounded, she'd never had someone she could rely on.

Glancing around the kitchen, she gulped down her glass of wine as if it were a soft drink. She'd built this house, on the outskirts of Houston's Memorial area, just after Mike had left. Early in their marriage they had designed it together—their dream home.

Every room in the U-shaped structure had a wall of glass that overlooked the patio and pool in the center. A small atrium in the living area made looking at the patio seem like gazing through a jungle to the oasis beyond. That had been her idea, and it was effective. Even Mike had said so when he came over—just one time—to pick up some belongings. Knowing Mike was impressed had given her a good feeling for a while.

Then she'd realized that he'd been fascinated, but not been saddened not to have been here during the planning stage. He hadn't regretted leaving her for her sister. He'd simply complimented her on achieving her dream, telling her he'd known she'd do it, with or without him. And then he'd left, looking more than eager to return to Cora.

She'd accomplished her goal of showing him what she could do. She'd shown him how successful she was, how much money she could command in her job. And she was still alone.

She looked around. Was this house a monument to revenge? She hadn't thought so at the time, but now she wasn't so sure. She'd lived for the day when Mike would see it and regret not having stayed with her. But he'd never done that.

Still the tears refused to fall.

With another glass of wine in her hand, though by now her head was pounding, Carolyn walked slowly into the bedroom, drew the drapes and stretched out on the king-size bed. Maybe everything would be fine again when she woke up.

Tony's image flashed into her head just seconds before she drifted off. She smiled back at it, as if recognizing an old friend.

She was in a deep sleep when her hands clenched around the extra pillow and brought it close. She never even heard herself crying in her sleep.

3

TONY DROPPED the Houston telephone directory onto his desk, leaned back in the overstuffed, corduroy chair and slipped off his reading glasses. He rubbed his eyes, then stared out through French doors that led to the patio. It was twilight, and the setting sun shone through tall pines and oaks, dappling the patio, making shadows move and play against the gray concrete. It was his favorite time of day, when he usually relaxed, had a drink and sat outside to say hello to the night.

He hadn't indulged in his favorite ritual lately.

It had been two months since he'd sold his business and retired from the everyday, working world. Two long months. Since then he'd grown a ponytail, something that proclaimed him an outlaw in the corporate world. He'd also invested the proceeds of the sale, making sure he would have a nice income for the rest of his life.

He felt satisfied with both results and was looking around for another, less stressful, business to get involved with. But there was no hurry. Since there was no pressure on him to earn his living, he could take his time, make sure that whatever he went into would be right for him.

Friends invited him out, but he didn't enjoy group socializing. He never had. One-on-one had always seemed more fun to him, especially if the other one was a beautiful woman.

Lately most of Tony's thoughts had been caught up in the memory of a blond woman with doe-brown eyes and a deep, inner sadness that had touched his soul.

There were over three hundred people with the last name of Perkins; and there was more than one way to spell the name. He couldn't remember whether the hotel slip had said "Perkins" or "Perkens." Whenever he had a spare fifteen minutes or so, he would call five or six at a time. Until recently, he hadn't had much spare time. Even though the deal had been closed, there had still been a lot of minor details to attend to. But he was making progress. So far he had called all the "Ens" in the phone book. Now he was dialing "Ins."

There was also a chance she had an unlisted number. Or she could be listed under another name. He knew most women didn't put their first names in the directories because they didn't want crank calls. But wouldn't she be listed by her initials? What if Carolyn was really her middle name?

He'd already called the hotel in Corpus Christi, but they had refused to give him any help at all. He sighed.

It didn't matter. He would call every damn Perkins in the book until he found the one he wanted.

If he batted zero at both of these pursuits, then he'd hire a private investigator to track her down. Certainly it couldn't be that hard to find her. She wasn't deliberately trying to hide her trail.

He'd try one more number before calling it quits for the night. When an answering machine picked up the call, his heart jumped into his throat.

It was Carolyn's voice. He was sure of it. No other voice could send lightning searing down his spine like that. Once her short message was over, he carefully hung up and stared at the number in the book, then painstakingly copied down both the number and the address. Once more he stared out the French doors.

He'd found her. Now what?

His phone rang, but Tony let the answering machine pick it up. A woman's sexy voice came across the line. "Hi, Tony, I don't know if you remember me, but my name is Shara and we met at Charles's party last month. There's a group of us over at the Ritz Carlton Hotel for drinks, and I was voted as most likely to persuade you to join us. We'll be here for the rest of the evening. Join us, won't you?" The machine clicked off.

He remembered Shara. She looked a little like Carolyn, which was probably why he'd been drawn to her. There was no doubt in his mind that Shara was impressed by what his friends had to say about him. She probably thought he was even wealthier than he was. But it didn't matter. No one had interested him since Carolyn entered his life.

But the only woman he wanted to impress with his prowess in business wasn't in a position to understand his importance in the world of finance. Carolyn wasn't with him, so he couldn't impress her with anything. He chuckled ruefully.

For the past two months his every thought had led him back to Carolyn. Now that he'd found her, his quest was almost over. He had given up on the idea of revenge—his reaction to her had been too strong. Yes, he wanted her to discover what she had missed by running away from him but it was more important to know if the chemistry between them still existed. What if that certain something had only been a figment of his over-active imagination? What if they hated each other? Or worse yet! What if there was no spark, no magic between them?

That did it. He stood and headed toward the bedroom. He could be dressed and with friends in an hour. It didn't match being able to see Carolyn in person and testing his reaction, but he needed more time to figure out what he would do when he finally met her again, face-to-face....

Less than an hour later Tony was leaning against the Ritz Carlton's long, mahogany bar. A three-piece combo played a shade too loudly on one corner of the dance floor. He was marginally bored with the conversation of the company, but being here was better than staying at home and rehashing a one-night stand that had apparently only impressed him.

Shara's flawlessly made-up face stared at him as if she'd just discovered fire. Even though he wasn't interested, it soothed his male ego to be sought after like this. Especially when Caro—

Tony tried to keep the last thought at bay. Anything to do with Carolyn right now was dangerous, robbing him of the enjoyment of the moment. He was in the company of a beautiful woman who obviously wanted to be with him. Thinking of someone else who, after making love with him all night long, had escaped from him at the first opportunity, was pointless. Now that he knew where Carolyn was, he could come to terms with the situation.

He smiled into Shara's eyes, wondering what the hell she was talking about, then glanced around the room as he sipped his drink. She was a very nice girl, but her ramblings bored him to death.

Suddenly every nerve in his body felt as if it were in Antarctica. Carolyn stood at the other end of the bar, a still-full glass of something with a twist of lime in her hand as she smiled and nodded at some well-dressed young man Tony wanted to punch out.

Her hair was pulled back and up from her face, and a floppy, black bow curled around the back of her slim neck. The style showed off pearl earrings, flawless skin and a profile even more beautiful than he remembered. She wore an expensive, pearl-gray suit that was strictly tailored. A black blouse with a waterfall-draped neckline was her only concession to femininity. His gaze narrowed. Her body language told him she was bored to tears.

He gave Shara a broad smile. "Would you excuse me for a moment? I see an old friend I must say hello to." Without waiting for an answer, he walked toward Carolyn, not stopping until he stood directly in front of her. She didn't notice him at first; she was too intent on looking at the liquid in her glass and nodding her head in agreement with whatever her companion was pontificating about. Then, as if she sensed him, she looked up, directly into his eyes.

The world dropped away. Her eyes widened in surprise, warming instantly in recognition. Tony felt warmth grow into heat; sensual memories awakened and were replayed. His throat tightened with need. The look in her eyes had answered at least half his questions.

Any speeches he might have dreamed up and rehearsed to impress her fled. Instead, he smiled. "Aren't you going to ask me to dance?"

The rose hue tinting her cheeks was absolutely beautiful. The man with her stopped talking, turning his head toward Tony. He bet he'd see irritation in the stranger's eyes, but didn't give a damn.

"Would you care to dance?" Carolyn asked softly.

He repeated what he'd said the night they met. "Are you talking to me?"

She nodded, a slow smile tilting her lips.

Without another word, Tony took her hand and led her onto the dance floor. Once there, she came into his arms as if coming home. Their steps still matched perfectly. He remained silent, waiting for her to say something, anything. He was surprised when, although she danced compliantly, she kept her silence. They were clearly both unwilling to break the spell.

Just like the first time, one song drifted into another. Tony kept going, wondering for the first time what would happen when the music speeded up or stopped. He didn't want to let her go, didn't want her to leave his arms.

She had lost weight, though her suit jacket hid the fact that her figure was even more slender than it had been two months ago. He could feel her rib bones. Was she working too hard, or was something else the problem?

A protective urge, primitive and strong, washed over him. He wanted to do more than comfort. He wanted to protect her from whatever was eating at her. As a matter of fact, he wanted *her*. Period. He wondered if anyone would try to stop him if he simply picked Carolyn up and carried her away, caveman style.

Carolyn's fingers brushed the nape of his neck, curling lightly under his ponytail, and his breathing stopped. It took him a while to begin breathing again.

"God, I missed you." He was surprised he'd spoken his thought aloud.

He felt her stiffen slightly. "Did you?"

"Yes." He pressed on. "What about you? Did you miss me? Us?"

He could almost feel her searching for a way out. "We weren't an 'us' long enough to become a habit."

It was a neat sidestep, and it made him mad that she was so easily able to take it, while he felt like a tongue-tied kid. "Do you do that often?"

She brought her head back and stared at him. "What?"

He knew he was going for shock value, but her control made him damned angry. "Pick up men in bars, make love to them, and then run off in the light of dawn."

She pulled away as if she'd been struck. Her face blazed red, then white. He felt her every muscle tighten. "If I didn't hate scenes, I'd slap your face right this minute and walk off the floor. Instead, I'll allow you the courtesy of walking me back to my purse."

"Don't get our roles confused," he said dryly, surprised by his own flaring anger. "I was the embarrassed jerk left holding the bag the last time."

Carolyn tried again to pull away, but he tightened his hold. "I was wrong," she finally muttered through clenched teeth. "Both times."

"How so?"

"When I first met you, I thought you were someone of value. For a moment this time, I thought I'd been right."

"Lady, you pack a punch!" Tony exclaimed.

"And you're more outrageous than I could ever believe. Do you honestly believe you can try this here? I have friends I can call if you don't let me go."

"Not until I apologize." He loosened his grip, wishing he'd kept a better rein on his temper. "I'm sorry."

She wasn't going to forgive him quickly. "Don't expect me to excuse you."

"Why not?"

"I've toughened over the years. Besides, I don't excuse any man with a ponytail. You're in the wrong place for that. Most of the people here are ambitious and hardworking, career men and women not old hippies."

"I could buy and sell half of these guys. I've done business with a quarter of them. Who's to say I can't wear anything I damn well please?"

"You're impossible!"

"Outrageous," he corrected softly.

Her mouth quirked, but he wasn't sure if it was a smile or simple irritation. He couldn't tell if she was irritated by the length of his hair or with herself for liking it. After all, she had stroked his hair while they'd been dancing.

He suddenly realized he didn't want to fight. Not about where she'd been or why he'd let his hair grow long. He just wanted to be with her.

"I have an earring that belongs to you."

Carolyn hesitated. "Diamond?"

He nodded.

"Where did you find it?"

"On the floor in your hotel room, when I returned to tell you how much meeting you had mattered to me. Instead, I found you had fled, leaving behind your diamond earring and my business card. You must have been in quite a hurry." He finally voiced the thought that hadn't been out of his mind these past two months. "Or was there a husband waiting in the wings, expecting his loving wife to return to his arms?"

He hadn't meant to accuse her of anything, hadn't meant to attack her again. He only wanted to hold her, convince her that they were good together and should try to begin a relationship. Instead, he had hurt her feelings, then insulted her.

Luckily, she appeared to understand that he wasn't acting out of anger anymore. She sighed and the stiffness left her body. "No husband. I just had something personal to do."

"What was it that could make you leave in less than a half hour after I did?" he asked. "A sudden case of guilt? A wedding? A death? Or was it just business as usual?"

"A funeral."

Tony had asked the question only because he hadn't expected that answer. If he continued on this path, he'd be apologizing to her all night long. "I'm sorry. As far as you're concerned, it seems I can't say anything right tonight. I know how painful an occasion like that can be. Was it someone close?"

"Close enough."

He took that to be a topic that was closed—for now. "My condolences."

"Thank you." She stopped dancing. "Will you please loosen your grip now?"

He hadn't realized just how tightly he'd been holding her. Reluctantly he did as she asked. He stared down; she was even more beautiful than he remembered. His memory hadn't been as accurate as he'd thought. "Better?"

She smiled, and the sight warmed his insides. "Better."

The slow music went into a staccato, Latin tempo, and Tony reluctantly dropped his hands. Carolyn turned, leading the way to her crowd and her drink.

Tony escorted her back. He wanted to stay with her, to be with her, but it was obvious Carolyn didn't feel that way.

Giving the group a curt nod, he left Carolyn and returned to Shara, who smiled with delight. He smiled back and asked her to dance. But dancing with Shara wasn't enough to block out the memory of Carolyn. For reasons he didn't want to delve into, he felt as if he were cheating now.

He spent the rest of the evening talking to his friends. He laughed at jokes he hardly heard, told one or two himself, shared experiences he'd had at work, had another drink and grinned a lot.

But all the time he was aware of Carolyn's every move. She seemed to be looking at him as often as he tried not to pay attention to her. It salved his ego to know that she was as aware of his presence as he of hers.

Not until he was ready to leave did he feel a sense of satisfaction. Carolyn was wending her way around the crowded bar until she stood in front of him.

"How do I reach you?" she asked quietly.

He tried to look surprised. "For what?"

Carolyn glanced at Shara, then leaned toward him and spoke in a whisper. "You know. My lost item?"

Tony leaned against the bar. It was clearly killing her to have anyone know he had such a personal item in his possession.

"Oh, you mean your earring?" His tone was innocent, and he kept his eyes wide.

Carolyn's eyes flashed lightning. "That's the one," she said sweetly, apparently no longer caring who heard. "The one you found when you illegally entered the room I'd checked out of."

He gave her credit for the shoot-down. But now that he had her attention, he wasn't about to lose control. "You can follow me home and I'll get it for you."

Staring him straight in the eye, she didn't miss a beat. "When?"

Tony glanced at his watch. He'd been fed up with the party scene for the past ten minutes, but wasn't willing to leave until she gave him some sort of acknowledgment. "Fifteen minutes?"

Her gaze hardened, and for a moment he wondered if she could read him so easily. She nodded curtly. "Okay. I'll meet you at the valet parking, then."

He watched her walk back to her friends. For reasons he couldn't begin to delve into, Carolyn was an important part of his life. She was in his thoughts, his feelings, and he didn't know why or how. He wasn't sure she felt even an inkling of the same thing.

Excusing himself at last, Tony walked out of the bar and down the hall to the valet parking station. He handed over his ticket and waited, not for his car, but for Carolyn. He deliberately hadn't looked at her as he left, but he'd bet his last dollar that she wasn't far behind him.

The doors behind him opened and he heard the familiar click of her high heels. He refused to look around. From the fragrance of her perfume, he knew that Carolyn was standing next to him.

When the valet brought his gray Mercedes-Benz to the front of the driveway, Tony took her elbow and guided her toward it.

"I'll take my own car and follow you," she protested, resisting.

"I'll bring you back."

She still balked. "That's too much trouble."

"Trust me," he said firmly. "It's no trouble at all. We'll only be a few minutes. I live ten minutes from here."

Visibly reluctant, she stepped into the car, sliding across the plush, leather seats. Tony closed her door with a satisfied snap and walked around to the driver's side, tipping the valet before getting in.

The engine purred as he pulled out and headed for home. She sat quietly beside him; it felt as if she belonged there. Although she was no doubt unused to sitting in a passenger seat, she was as relaxed as her workaholic nature could allow—for now. He promised himself to change that.

Carolyn's attention was fixed on the house in front of her as he pulled into his driveway and pushed the button to open the gates. It was not a large house, as far as homes went in the West University area, but it was a gracious structure. Georgian in design, with two stories, it was painted in shades that went from smoky to a deep gray, with touches of white and splashes of zinnia red and impatiens pink for color. The outside lighting beautifully emphasized the style—and the For Sale sign in the front yard.

"How lovely," Carolyn murmured.

He pulled up at the front walk and turned off the engine. "Thank you."

"You're selling it."

"I don't need it anymore." It was the truth.

"Why?"

"Because it's too big to rattle around in, and I spend too much time on its upkeep, when I want to lie back and enjoy."

"It's a family home," she said quietly.

"I don't have a family anymore."

Her head swiveled toward him, her eyes large and luminous in the dark. "What happened?"

"My son died in a boating accident ten years ago. He was eight. My wife died of cancer six years ago. I think she lost the will to fight when our son died."

She reached across the seat and touched his arm, her expression gentle. "I'm so sorry. You must have been devastated."

He nodded. In her eyes there was a shadow of the pain he'd felt. "I was. But the saying that time heals all wounds is right. Sooner or later you pick up and go on with life. Sometimes only because life forces you into that position. It demands you pay bills, mow the lawn or work for a living."

"That doesn't make the hurting go away."

"Nothing makes the memories and regrets go away, Carolyn. But the hurting turns into a dull ache that overwhelms you only occasionally, instead of all the time. And then, someday you meet someone else and realize there's a future."

"Oh? Like what?" Her tone had suddenly grown distant. She could have been asking the time. He knew that quirk. It helped her keep her own anguish at bay.

"Well, whatever you experience at twenty is never quite as deep as what you experience at thirty. Whatever happens in your thirties isn't quite as traumatic or as unmanageable later."

Carolyn folded her hands in her lap and stared at him. He missed her touch. "Is this the old pep talk that says everything gets better with time and I'm just too young to appreciate that fact?"

"How old are you?"

She didn't hesitate. "Thirty-five. How old are you?"

"Forty-two."

"So young for so much. You must have been a boy genius or born to wealth."

"Neither. Just a hard worker, like yourself."

"A hard worker with a ponytail?"

He shrugged. "Why not?"

"Because business twenty years ago wouldn't allow that."

"Ahh, but I only grew it in the last three months. And I'm not in the business world anymore. I can do as I damn well please. And I mean to do just that."

She smiled, then laughed, tilting her head as if studying him. "I bet you've always been the rebel type."

"Sounds like one of those silly personal ads: 'Rebel, ready to do outrageous deeds, as long as they're for the love of a beautiful woman.'"

The muted, outdoor lights shot gold threads through her hair, shadowing her face into even more dramatic planes. Tony reached out and touched her cheek and outlined her full bottom lip with his thumb, his narrowed gaze fascinated by the parting of her lips and the gleam of pearl-white teeth. He ached to kiss her.

But he denied himself. "You're so beautiful."

Her lashes drifted down to resemble soot smudges on her creamy skin. For a moment he thought she would dispute his statement. But then she seemed to swallow the words that had almost begun to come forth and said what he wanted to hear. "Thank you."

"You're welcome." The inside of the car fairly sang with the tension between them. "Have dinner with me tomorrow night."

"I can't. I have a business meeting."

At least she'd given a reason for her refusal. But that reason wasn't strong enough for Tony. "Cancel it. Meetings are a dime a dozen in the business world. Slow dining, on wonderful food, with company that lets your blood flow hot, is what you need."

"Spoken like a true gourmet—and a lech." Her voice was a mere whisper against his thumb; lightning zigzagged down his spine at the thought of placing his mouth where that thumb had been resting.

"Say yes. Eight o'clock," he demanded, with every ounce of his being.

She must have picked up the vibrations. "Nothing else?"

"Like what?"

"You know what. We won't wind up like we did the last time, Tony. Never. It was a mistake. One I won't make again."

"You certainly know how to make a compliment."

"I'm sorry, but it was, and we both know it. I can't let that happen again."

"Never is such a long time." She looked as if she would protest and he smiled. "But certainly not this time. Just dinner and good conversation. I promise I'll play the gentleman, as long as you play the proper lady. But I warn you, one slip, and all the rules go by the wayside."

Her smile lighted his heart. "I think you might be the devil in disguise. You charm and wheedle your way into a woman's confidence, then plead not guilty if anything happens."

He grinned. "I know. Isn't it great? And you're willing to take the blame."

"Thanks," she replied dryly. "I'm not sure having to watch my behavior is worth a dinner, gourmet feast or not."

"Then don't pay any attention to your behavior," he told her firmly. "Just enjoy, and let's see where it leads."

The temptation was too great. He leaned forward and brushed her lips with his own. An electrical charge rolled through him, making him aware just how dark it was, how small the interior of the car, how much he wanted to take this woman, right now.

Instead, he pulled back and started the engine. Looking over his shoulder, he backed out of the driveway.

"What about my earring?"

"I'll give it to you tomorrow night. It's your bribe for going out with me."

"That's not fair."

He wouldn't admit that she wasn't safe from ravishment in his car a minute longer and that he was doing this for her, as well as to keep himself under control. "It's fair. You'd have lost the earring forever if I hadn't found it. Now that I've got it, I could get my ear pierced and wear it myself. Instead, I'm asking for an evening of dinner and conversation with you and I'll hold it hostage until then."

Her soft laughter filled the car like the finest perfume. He joined her, knowing that there were few perfect moments in life, and that this one would stick in his memory until he died.

For the moment, Tony Valentine had the opportunity he wanted. Now it was up to him to make Carolyn want to be with him again. It was up to him—and to the fates—to make things happen.

He'd take his chance. After all, the fates owed him one.

4

CAROLYN LAY IN BED, staring at the ceiling. When she'd first moved into the house, she'd placed small, whimsical stars all over her bedroom ceiling that glowed for the first ten or fifteen minutes after the lights went out. Going to bed and seeing them had given her a sense of peace. With everything in her life topsy-turvy she had needed their reassurance. She still did.

Tonight was no different. She seriously wondered about her sanity. She couldn't believe she had agreed to dinner! She had counted on *never* seeing Tony again. She had *planned* on never seeing him again!

She had made a mistake that night, one she wanted to forget. Now Tony was here to remind her, and she was having dinner with him!

She remembered the night she'd met him, reliving the regrets, self-doubt and overwhelming sadness that had ruled her. She might have had an excuse for what she'd done in tempting a stranger into her bed, but in this day and age, she should have had more control over herself. Instead, she played the game of sexual roulette. Never again, she promised herself.

But the memories of their behavior, their actions, tantalized her now like forbidden fruit, with their taste and texture. She'd tried to control her emotions and keep her mind on business, but it didn't always work. In fact, not an hour went by without some scene of the two of them talking, walking, or making love flashing into her head.

Tony was the most fascinating subject she could contemplate. But she didn't like it, not one bit. *No one* should take over her thoughts like that. She'd made up her mind years ago that the only ideas she'd allow herself to explore would be related to success.

After Mike had left her, her main focus had been on what her friends used to call The Best Revenge. "The best revenge is living well," they'd all said, and she'd believed it. She'd wanted Mike to regret leaving her, had wanted him to return to her, beg her forgiveness, so she could be sweet and magnanimous—and then turn him down flat. And she'd wanted Cora to know how it felt to lose someone you cared for, counted on and wanted to be with.

But when Tony entered her life for that one night, everything changed. She'd lost the dream of revenge on her sister and ex-husband she'd been carrying for the last four years.

She'd also lost her reason for working. That was the worst part. Aside from trying to come to terms with their deaths, she now also had to find something else to use as a goal, a focal point.

Perhaps, she told herself, that was why she'd begun thinking of Tony so often. Sadness at her loss would always be there. Maybe Tony was on her mind for another reason. Yes, that was it. She only thought of Tony because she had lost so much more than her family, she had lost her motivation for getting through daily living.

But now she understood all she needed to find was another goal. Then she'd stop thinking about the man with blue-gray eyes and a ponytail of sun-kissed brown hair that declared him an insurgent, a revolutionary, outside the business world. It was only a passing fancy on her part.

All she had to remember was that she wanted, needed, more than he could give her. She wanted everything: home, family, career, prestige, and a closeness to someone with similar goals and dreams.

Tony didn't seem to want more than a good meal and great sex. He didn't act as if he wanted to be her best friend, and that was what she needed most, right now. It was also the one thing she would never ask for.

She went to sleep on that thought.

THE FOLLOWING NIGHT, while waiting for Tony, she wondered if her assumptions hadn't been a wee bit naive.

Her nerves were so tense that she jumped when her doorbell rang. Finishing the glass of water she'd just poured, Carolyn forced herself to walk slowly to the front door and peek through the lens.

Hoping to see an agitated Tony waiting for her to open the door, she found a cool, calm Tony staring back at her, a small, sexy smile turning up the corners of his mouth. He was wearing a dark blue suit with a multi-colored, silk tie, his long hair pulled back.

She opened the door, knowing that delight at seeing him was shining in her eyes. "Hi," she said.

"Hi." His gaze ran appreciatively over her muted pink and blue silk dress, right down to the flare at the hem. "You're beautiful."

She laughed, feeling a buoyancy she hadn't experienced in years. "That's what you said the last time."

"I meant it then and I mean it now."

Carolyn dipped her head and bobbed in an imitation of a curtsy. "Thank you, kind sir." She opened the door wider. "Would you care for a drink before we go?"

"I'd love one," he said, stepping over the threshold. His gaze took in the wide, expansive hallway dressed in tans and summer whites and the two-tone, tiled floor. She saw his eyes take in all the detail, from the atrium to the courtyard and beyond, to the swimming pool. "Good design."

She could take full credit and did so. "Thank you, again."

"Did you design it?" he asked, walking toward the glass wall. "It's very unusual."

"Partially. But what was most important, I implemented it," she told him, unwilling to go further. "What would you like to drink?"

"Scotch and water will be fine," he said, still staring outside to the patio. "Was this your dream for a long time?"

"Yes." She didn't mean to sound short, but didn't want to talk about her reasons, about Mike.

High heels clicked on the tiled entry as she stepped to the wet bar and pulled the liquor bottle from the cabinet. She knew which question he would ask next and wished she could come up with a quick, snappy answer to avoid having to tell the story he plainly wanted to hear.

"Did you plan this house with your husband?"

"Ex-husband. Yes."

"Did he see its completion?"

She walked toward him holding out a glass. "Yes."

Accepting the drink, his gaze narrowed knowingly. "And you wish I'd shut up."

"Yes."

He stared into the golden-colored liquid, then back at her. "I told you my wife died six years ago, Carolyn.

Although we were happy together, there were several things that went unresolved. I now wish I'd said so many things to her when I had the chance. So I've learned to say *what* I want *when* I want. I live with fewer regrets that way."

Her heart skipped a beat, but she kept her expression blank. "Really."

Tony nodded. "And there are things I'd wished *she*'d said, but didn't."

If he'd set out to intrigue her, he'd succeeded. "Like what?"

As if choosing his words carefully, Tony stared pensively at the pool area, where the lights glowed softly enough to preserve the mystery of night. "I needed to hear that she understood, all the times I left her alone while I conducted business into the early-morning hours. That she wasn't hurt every time I turned down her request to do something together, in order to do something with business associates. That she loved me in spite of all my faults." He waited a moment. "That she forgave me for being human."

She felt his wish as if it were her own. Wasn't that exactly the way she'd felt at the funeral? Didn't she still feel that way? Without hesitating, she reached out and touched his arm. "I'm so sorry."

Tony's gaze was open and warm, with just a hint of the vulnerability she knew he felt. "Thanks. But I needed to apologize to her, too."

"For being a workaholic? Don't you think she understood that?"

"No. I think she tried, but even I didn't understand my own motives then, so how could she?"

Carolyn felt confused. "What's to understand? You worked hard to make a success of yourself. If that was a crime, no one would marry."

"If it was such a little thing, no one would be divorcing," Tony retorted. "The toughest spot in the world to be in is second to everything in your mate's life. That was my wife's position. I'd venture a guess that it was also your husband's."

"Ex-husband," Carolyn repeated stiffly, withdrawing her hand. "And neither my marriage nor my divorce are topics for discussion."

"Why not?" he asked calmly. "If you didn't learn something from that marriage, what's going to stop you from making the same mistake again?"

"*I* am." It was said with such conviction that Tony looked surprised. "I'll never marry again."

"Never is a long time, Carolyn. Too long to be alone for the rest of your life."

She'd already heard those arguments from her friends. They'd had no meaning then, nor did they now. "Maybe so, but no relationship will lead me to the altar again. Ever."

"That, my beautiful Carolyn, sounds like fear of commitment." His tone was dry, the corners of his mouth tilted up in a sexy smile.

"That, my handsome Tony, sounds like good advice to a man who already has enough regrets." Her tone parodied his.

"Touché," he murmured, apparently giving her credit for a direct hit. "I take it you've decided not to have children."

She shrugged her shoulders and looked in the other direction, unwilling to explore that topic. "If I want one, I could have one without a husband."

"But can you raise it and give it all the opportunities in life without a complete family?"

"Many families today are single-parent families."

"That's not ideal, Carolyn."

"Like many women, if I decide to have a family, I'll make the best of it." She hesitated a moment. "Sometimes, Tony, simply having a father isn't good enough."

He knew when to call off the discussion, and this was the time. "Good luck, then," Tony murmured.

He took another sip of his drink, then wandered out of the large entry and turned right, into the living room. "Mind if I take a tour? The house is so unusual, I'd like to see the layout."

"Of course," she said, following him as he mean-dered into the next room. Mexican tile marked the pathway between the room and the large expanse of glass wall that displayed the patio and pool. The sunken living room was cut off from the hall by pale cream carpeting. The upholstered furniture was also cream, accented with peach and jungle-green cushions. Pieces of art stood here and there. The colors and atmosphere blended with the world outside, making the room look even larger than it was.

"Beautiful."

"Thank you." She sounded formal but couldn't help it. Her gaze followed his, recognizing each object his eyes alighted on. Each item had been carefully chosen. At the time it had been fun, but the pleasure had faded rapidly when Mike didn't bother to notice the details she'd so painstakingly worked on.

Tony walked on to her study and Carolyn tensed. He glanced at her computer station and the small, note-book laptop that sat next to it, but never gave the chairs, desk, and small settee a second look. Instead, he focused on a painting behind her desk that she'd found years ago, long before the house was built. In cream, gray and black, it showed a little girl playing with a sailboat by a wooded stream. He stared at the picture for several minutes without saying a word.

Then he turned and walked the next few feet to the last room.

Carolyn stopped breathing. He was standing on the threshold of the master bedroom suite. He turned, and she saw his eyes widen. "Lady, you've got a hidden self. And it's marvelous," he finally muttered.

Once more, Carolyn saw the room through his eyes. Here the cream-colored carpet was covered with a massive, Oriental rug in shades of cream, tan, bronze and touches of forest green, while the walls were painted a rich cream and golden bronze. But here the bed was the principal feature. Standing opposite the large, sliding glass doors that led to the patio was a king-size canopy of bronze metal, draped in intertwined, white and cream gauze that looped around the top and sides. Piled against the headboard, on top of the vanilla-colored bedspread, were mounds of pillows.

At the foot of the bed was a bench-high chest of the same bronze, on which stood an arrangement of tall irises and a number of photos in ornate, silver and bronze frames. Against one wall a pickled-wood armoire stood stiffly, like a sentinel. In front of the glass wall were plants of all shapes and sizes, their green the perfect foil for the other colors. The light scent of flowers filled the room. Without a frill anywhere, the room was totally feminine and sensuous.

Carolyn blushed. She'd never really noticed before. "It's just a bedroom," she protested softly, not wishing to admit, even to herself, that it was a dream place for making love.

"A bedroom to dream and make love in," Tony said, equally softly, stopping in front of a Dali watercolor. "It's real."

"Yes." She was proud of that painting. Her girl-friends had never commented on it, had never known it wasn't a reproduction. No man other than Mike had ever seen it—until now.

"That had to have cost a pretty penny."

"A bonus check plus," she admitted, unwilling to give him too clear an idea of how good she was at her job.

"It represents a lot of effort and late-night paper-work."

"Of course." She smiled. He understood.

"It also means that you sleep alone in that beautiful bed."

She felt herself flush, but stood her ground. "How can you draw that conclusion?"

"Because you spent too many nights working late to earn that painting. If you'd played around, you wouldn't have had the time or dedication."

She wasn't used to feeling exposed. It wasn't a comfortable feeling. "You don't know that."

Tony walked toward her, not stopping until he was just inches away. He reached out and touched the side of her cheek with a lightly callused finger, drawing it down to her neck. A shiver of anticipation zinged through her, but she concealed it.

"I know." His whisper was as confirming as the look in his eyes. His hand dropped to his side.

He was right, she thought. He knew. When she opened her mouth to speak, the words came out as a soft, aching whisper. "Don't touch me."

His lips were too close for comfort. His breath was warm and scented with Scotch. "Why not, when everything I feel tells me to kiss you?"

"No."

"Yes." His lips came down slowly. He didn't touch her, but she was powerless to move away. Instead, she waited, craving the feel of his firm mouth on hers. She needed to know if her memories of them together were really dreams, conjured up in a lonely moment, or if she'd exaggerated his exquisite taste, sensual texture, and her own instant, inner response.

When his mouth covered hers, she stopped breathing again. Her body froze, then melted slowly into the magic of his kiss. Her lips softened, inviting him to explore further, and he took the invitation.

Carolyn's responses were as intense as on the night they'd met. What was worse, this time she craved more.

She didn't want the kiss to end, but to be the prelude to a night of lovemaking. When he pulled away, a chill of desolation washed over her.

"I just don't understand how so much chemistry can be in one kiss—and you don't want us to make love." His voice was low, rasping at every nerve ending.

"It was nice," she got out finally. She would not admit to more.

His deep chuckle echoed through the room. "Right," he drawled, stepping away from her and toward the door. "May I see the other side of the house, too?"

She swallowed hard, grasping for her composure. "Of course."

This time she led the way, out of the room and down the hall, past the living room and entry to the other side of the house, which began with her step-up dining room. Here the wall opposite the glass was mirrored.

Tony stopped and whistled softly. "Every guest gets a view."

"It only seems fair," she agreed, knowing she sounded far more complacent than she felt. Standing so close to him, all she could think of was how it felt to kiss him. Damn the man. Tony was disrupting her life.

Beyond the dining area lay the kitchen, with every modern appliance built into workstations. Two other bedrooms were down the hall, with a Hollywood bath between. Tony's cursory glance in that direction confirmed that he had found out what he wanted to know—she lived alone.

She placed her wineglass on the tile of the bar. "Well, now that you've seen the house, are you ready to go? I'm starving."

His blue-gray gaze snared hers. "What's the matter, Carolyn? Are you feeling awkward?"

Enough games, she thought, feeling irritation flare. He wanted the truth, it was time to give it to him. "I'm not used to having a man walk through my home, scrutinizing everything. It's an invasion of my privacy."

"So thank you for showing it to me." His smile bordered on the smug. He placed his glass next to hers. "Shall we go?"

Setting the burglar alarm, she led him outside. Tony opened the car door for her and she slipped inside. By the time he was in the driver's seat, she was embarrassed by her outburst, but wasn't sure what to say to ease the tension. Finally, she decided that the best thing she could do was keep quiet. He had apparently come to the same conclusion; they rode in silence.

Tony went to a small Mexican restaurant Carolyn had heard about, but had never been to before. There were no signs on the door, no windows on the front. The owners cared so little for advertising that they allowed news of their epicurean delights to travel by word of mouth. To Carolyn's knowledge it had been open for more than ten years. Apparently word of mouth wasn't a bad way to advertise.

Tony's name was on the reservations list and their table was ready. One appetizer after another was brought out for sampling, then they ordered their main course. By the time the dessert arrived, Carolyn was sure she'd never eat again. Sopaipillas, hot, pillow-shaped doughnuts, sprinkled with sugar and covered with honey, were presented with a flourish. Finding more room for the lighter-than-air dessert was hard, but Carolyn succeeded. So did Tony.

Even though the food was wonderful, Carolyn was distracted whenever she looked at Tony. The expression in his eyes was slumberous, indecently reminding her of all the things they'd said and done while making love. One glance from him and she flushed at the vivid memory. When he smiled that slow, sexy smile, her body reacted just as it had on the night they met. She didn't know if he was toying with her on purpose, but wanted to tell him to stop. If she did, however, he'd realize just how much he was affecting her, so she refused to give him that satisfaction.

After dinner they drove to the tall, outdoor wall of water on the grounds of the Transco Tower in the Galleria area. High heels held safely in her hand, Carolyn walked by his side across the grass to the concrete seats, listening to the gentle song of the water as it flowed down and into a narrow pool. Several couples were milling around. A few tourists with children watched the water and talked quietly. It was a restful place.

Tony rested his foot on the seat beside her, arms braced on his leg. He looked serious, even solemn. "What happened when your husband died?" he asked quietly.

She was startled by the question. Of all the things she had expected him to ask, that wasn't it, but she realized that she wanted to tell him. Maybe it would help her to put the whole episode behind her. "Mike was my ex-husband. Somehow these connections aren't always severed cleanly when you divorce. In this case, there was a lot of unfinished business between us."

He reached out and cupped her cheek. "Don't keep it locked up, Carolyn, or it will devour you. Grief needs to be faced. Only then will the pain eventually disappear."

A lump formed in her throat and she swallowed hard. She'd waited over three months to cry. She didn't want to cry now. A stranger's compassion shouldn't be the trigger for her emotions. But it was too late. "That's not it," she found herself saying. "My husband divorced me to marry my sister."

The silence stretched so far that Carolyn thought her nerves would snap. When she finally looked up, she found Tony's eyes filled with understanding. "So that's it."

Unwilling to reveal any more of her vulnerability, she stared at the shoes in her hands and shrugged. "That's it."

"You poor baby."

His low, gravelly tone worked like salve on her burning hurt. Carolyn took a deep breath and felt the hurt turn slowly into an ache. He knew now, yet he wasn't asking all the questions she didn't want to answer. And he hadn't walked away. She waited. Maybe he wouldn't now, but might later.

"No wonder you were in such bad shape."

His hand smoothed the side of her neck, and she found herself arching, like a cat being stroked. However good it felt to be vindicated for her behavior on that first night, it also felt achingly wonderful to be touched again. It had been so long....

Carolyn opened her eyes. Panic at being this close to him, at needing his touch, flowed through her and she stood abruptly. "It's getting late. I have to go."

Tony frowned. "Or you turn into a pumpkin?"

She forced a bright, cheery smile. "No, but I have to visit an account in Oklahoma and I need to get the files ready."

"Why?"

"So I can do a good job when I get there." She took pains to make her tone more than indulgent. Didn't he know the first thing about business?

"Wouldn't it be cheaper to get everything ready and then set up a conference call for an all-day project? Between the fax machine and the files, you could get all the problems worked out in one day, rather than being gone for two or three and have the company carry those travel expenses."

"I don't think so," she said doggedly. "That doesn't get the job done as well as on-the-job snooping."

"Is this an audit?"

"No." Before he could ask more questions that would put her on the defensive again, she returned to the original topic. "So I still have to get some sleep."

"Don't shut me out, Carolyn."

"I wouldn't dream of it," she said sweetly, already regretting how much she had told him. "But it's time to go home. You were promised dinner, not the entire evening."

Tony's hand dropped to his side, all emotion erased from his face. "Of course."

Immediately she felt his withdrawal. She'd wanted it. So why did she feel so ... empty?

They walked to the car in silence. Within minutes, Tony had parked the car in her driveway and was holding open the door.

Carolyn walked stiffly into the house. "Thank you for a lovely evening," she said, dismissing him.

"I'm not leaving yet, Carolyn."

Anger flared again and she gave him a scathing look, then turned her back on him with a shrug. "Suit yourself. But when you leave, please twist the lock on the front door."

"Come back. Talk to me." His tone was so sympathetic that she almost turned around. But her strength returned quickly. Ignoring Tony, she continued down the tiled passageway toward her room. She walked straight in, dropped her purse at the foot of the bed and stepped into the bathroom, shutting the door quietly behind her.

Carolyn dimly registered her shaking hands as she took her hand off the knob. Moving with determination, she turned the shower tap on, then began stripping.

He would go, she told herself. He would leave and she would be alone, able to cope with her emotions once more. He wouldn't stand there and wait for her—wait to give her the comfort she so desperately needed. She shook off the thought; she was the strong one. She didn't need help. If they had just met a month or two later, she might have been in better control and able to handle a date with Tony. But not yet. Obviously.

Standing naked in front of the mirror, she replayed the night they'd spent together and wondered what it would be like to make love with Tony just once more. Then she shook her head resolutely and stepped into the shower stall. Hot water sluiced her body, washing away the surface tension. She knew that nothing would wash away the knots in her stomach, nothing, unless Tony disappeared from her life.

She turned off the water and grabbed a towel, scrubbing her skin pink. Then, taking a terry bathrobe from the back of the door, she put it on, like armor against whatever was on the other side.

Praying that he had left, she opened the door and stepped into the bedroom. Tony stood at the foot of her bed, a framed collage of photos in his hand. His expression was shocked.

"My God, Carolyn!" he said softly. "You must have been devastated."

Her heart sank to her toes. The collage was of Cora and herself. Growing up the two of them had done everything together. They had tried fishing for the first time and each of them had caught one. They had gone to an exhibit in Dallas and had their picture taken in front of one of the tomb statues. They had climbed a steep, Mexican pyramid and done a Rocky dance on top. There were numerous other shots of deeds they'd accomplished together. The last picture was one of her family when Carolyn was eighteen. In the background, their mom and dad were seated together beside a tree separate from the family, as usual. Carolyn and Cora were both sitting on tree limbs, while Ed leaned against the trunk, a wide grin on his face. They were all dressed in their Sunday best. Someone had cracked a joke—the irrepressible Cora, she thought—so they actually had genuine smiles on their faces. But she and Cora had tilted their heads together, and love and laughter showed in their faces.

"Don't," she said, her voice a rough whisper.

"Cora had to be your best friend."

"Please leave."

Instead, Tony replaced the frame on the chest and walked toward her; he took her into his arms and held her against his strength. Tears burned her eyes, and a lump formed in her throat until she couldn't swallow anymore. Suddenly, the dam broke.

All the hurt, the heartache, the disbelief over her wrecked marriage and lost sister rose to the surface, almost drowning her in the sea of tears she'd held back for the past three months. Sobs shook her body. She curled her fingers into fists, clenching his jacket and shirt in the palm of her hands. She knew that she hurt, but Tony was here, and she found some measure of satisfaction and comfort in that.

She felt him pick her up and carry her to the bed. Then they were both lying on top of the comforter, Tony cradling her in his lap, his voice a low crooning in her ears. Carolyn wept.

5

THE TICKING CLOCK on the bedside table read a little after 1:00 a.m. when Tony eased the sleeping Carolyn off his shoulder and allowed her to snuggle deeper into the pillows. She sighed, hiccuped, then rested once more.

In sleep she looked soft and lost, a lot like a little girl who'd just found out there was no Santa. A line of concentration, perhaps sadness, furrowed her brow. He wanted to get back into bed and hold her again until she smiled. She deserved to be able to lean on someone occasionally—everyone did. Most of all, he wanted to protect her from her memories. But he couldn't. She wouldn't allow him to come close enough to try.

So he did what he could. Tony took the bottom corner of the comforter and flipped it over to cover her. He pulled out his clean handkerchief and unfolded it, placing it, with her diamond earring on top, upon the chest.

Breathing one more light kiss onto her brow, Tony forced himself to leave her place and drive home.

The streets glistened with dampness from the Houston humidity and a light rain that had fallen while Carolyn slept in his arms. Tony shifted in his seat, remembering all too well the softness of her body against his, the hands that had touched him, seeking comfort, her warm breath, as it had wafted over his skin, and the aroma that surrounded her head with a halo of perfume.

Until now, he'd never believed in love at first sight. Carolyn had changed his mind on that score. Carolyn had changed his mind on a lot of things, and it was all because he loved her.

Who would have thought that he'd fall in love again? After six years of waiting for someone to step into his life, he had given up. Besides, he'd told himself, loving once was enough. Twice was for youngsters. Now he knew that that kind of thinking was an excuse for not having someone to love.

And love her Tony did. He loved Carolyn with everything he had in him. What surprised him was the depth of his feeling. When he'd first married, he'd been a young man with a young man's idealistic dreams. This time he had the depth that came from experiencing the reality of life, that was what made his love for her so much deeper, more intense. It also made him understand how hard it was going to be to get her to love him in return.

Nonetheless, he'd learned tonight that he had something of importance to offer her. He'd been through what she was suffering. He could help her.

And if she fell in love with him in the process, he'd be happy. For now, he'd settle for having a part of her life as his own.

He fancied he craved the same things she did, and none of them had to do with a career. Work was simply her excuse for not getting involved. He had a feeling that what she really wanted was to do something praiseworthy, and to revive her strong sense of family. She wanted someone she loved to praise her.

Unbeknownst to her, she'd shown those parts of her inner self by her tendency to workaholism and the air of loneliness that seemed to surround her.

Sooner or later, Carolyn would see the wisdom of being with him. She had to or he would never be happy. And no one would make her as happy as he could.

CAROLYN DRAGGED HERSELF through the week's work. Her crying bout had left her feeling drugged, lethargic and bone-dry. Although the last thing she wanted to think about was Tony's visit, she had no choice.

And she missed Tony. She didn't know when he'd left, but he hadn't been there at four in the morning when she awoke, wanting to cuddle. Cuddle? she asked herself derisively. Was that what she was now calling making passionate love? All the same, if he'd been here and she could have pretended to still be half-asleep, she would have had the excuse she needed to make love again without committing herself.

But he wasn't here and she missed him. She was also slightly embarrassed by the way she'd behaved. Until now she'd always been the strong one, not even crying in front of the family, let alone a stranger.

The one thing she was sure of was that she hadn't driven him away. She wasn't sure how she knew that, but she did.

It was hard to believe that he'd given her such a complete feeling of calm and contentment after she'd been so upset. Any other sane male might have taken one look and run, not wanting to get emotionally involved with a woman who fell apart at the first sound of a kind word. Not Tony.

She missed him even more when she found her diamond earring. It reminded her of their meeting in Corpus Christi and the overwhelming flow of emotions that had swept over her there, too. The earring told her that he was a man of his word. He could easily have forgotten his promise to return it, then used the jewel as more leverage for another date. But he hadn't. He'd remembered and followed through.

He called every evening for the next week, putting to rest all fears and anxieties about his feelings toward her. He was kind and warm and steady—just the same.

They talked for a long time and that helped assuage the loneliness she'd been feeling lately. Neither of them mentioned her emotional collapse. Neither suggested meeting again. Their telephone conversations were just a wonderful, sharing time that ended each hectic day, bringing a smile to her lips and a feeling of contentment.

Later that week, she decided Tony was habit-forming. No matter how much she told herself not to look forward to his calls, she found herself waiting for the phone to ring, growing anxious until it did and she heard Tony's voice.

HER WAYWARD THOUGHTS were brought short when her boss, Jeff Harden, poked his head into her doorway. In his late fifties, he still thought of himself as boyish, and dressed and acted the role. "Will you be checking on the Broylen account next week?"

Dropping her hand from her temple, she tried to smile. "Yes. It's my last road trip for the month."

"Where to?"

"Santa Fe. That account hasn't been personally tended for the last two quarters."

"Okay, but we need help with the files that Cindy left. Since she quit, no one's had the time to check out her business. Will you be able to handle that for me?" He gave the winning smile that was supposed to change her mind about turning him down. It did, but not because she was eager for work. Carolyn was eager for a promotion.

"All right," she promised. "I'll see what I can do." She wrote a note, reminding herself to grab the stack of files from the secretary, then stuck it onto her already well-filled attaché case. She nodded. "It's half done."

He gave her another flash of his smile. "Thanks. I thought I could count on you." He disappeared as quickly as he'd come.

It never failed. Jeff always managed to dump more work onto her. And if *he* didn't think she did enough, she reasoned, then the other partners certainly wouldn't think so, either. The only problem was that lately she'd begun to weary of being "rewarded" by being given even more work.

She brushed those rebellious thoughts aside and got back to work. Whining wouldn't bring her a partnership.

The afternoon seemed too short, with not enough time to do most of the things she had on her list. By seven she was tired, more than ready to go home to a light dinner. She'd finish off the paperwork while listening to the stereo until Tony called. Tony's call had become her reward for everything she did during the day.

She grabbed her briefcase and headed for the door and the parking lot. Halfway to her car she noticed a familiar one, parked behind hers. It was Tony's.

She walked on as casually as she could, fighting the urge to show her delight at seeing him.

"Hi," she said as he stepped forward, wearing well-worn, molded jeans and a blue chambray shirt that showed off his golden tan. His sun-streaked brown hair was once again neatly tied back in a ponytail with a leather thong. He looked sexy and intensely masculine. "What are you doing here?"

"Taking you on a picnic."

"Isn't it a little late in the day?"

He shook his head. "Not for an evening meal. This way the ants aren't invited."

The weight of her briefcase reminded her of the work she still had to do. "I'm sorry. I promised I'd get some work done tonight."

"And is that any different from the work you did last week or the week before?"

"Similar," she admitted, chin held high.

"And will it be the same next week?" he added, raising one brow in an intimidating gesture. "And the next?"

"Similar."

He smiled slowly. Wickedly. Light dimples creased his cheeks. "In that case . . ." He opened the passenger door of his car. "You're coming with me. Everything else can wait. Right now, life is calling."

Carolyn weighed the attaché case in her hand against the marshmallow softness of the leather seats and the company of the man she most wanted to be with. All the way down in the elevator, she'd been thinking about his phone call. Now he was here. "Let me put this in my trunk."

Two minutes later they were on the freeway, driving west into the last of the sun's rays.

Even though her conscience told her she should feel guilty for leaving her work behind, Carolyn's heart was light. Tony took her hand into his and, with a smile, kept driving toward the sunset. She reveled in being with him until she realized she hadn't even asked where they were going. She didn't really care, not as long as she was with Tony, but asked, anyway. "Where are we going?"

"To a little park in the center of a small town I know. They have benches and soft lights and even an occasional, cool breeze."

He was right. The town was small, and the park was smaller, heavily treed, but well lighted, with lamps on every curve and corner. Old men concentrated on boards of chess and checkers at the tables. Children played tag in the clearing. Mothers strolled along the paths with toddlers.

Tony unpacked the wicker basket. A red-checkered, oilskin tablecloth and napkins came first, then the food; large poor boys in thick, crisp-crusted bread. Enormous, puckering pickles, several different kinds of potato and corn chips, fresh watermelon and cantaloupe balls in a see-through container, and a bottle of sunshine-bright orange juice completed the meal. Last was a bottle of champagne.

"To make you a Mimosa," Tony explained with a twinkle in his eye. "I want you relaxed, not all uptight about the work you have to do."

Carolyn laughed and gave him a mock salute. "Yes, sir!"

They ate in a companionable way that she had never experienced before. It was casual, sassy, fun and relaxing—and yet exciting. Anyone could easily have taken them for good friends rather than lovers. Tony was witty and easy to talk to and broached several topics that were nonthreatening: movies, books, and funny things that had happened in his field of business.

Darkness descended and most of the mothers and children went home. Having finished their games of chess or checkers, some of the old gentlemen left, too. Still Tony and Carolyn talked. Although the basket had been repacked, they lingered with the last Mimosa.

Tony's hand covered hers as if it were the most natural thing in the world. But his thumb searching out the soft parts of her palm made her sensually aware of his maleness. It wasn't blatant, just there. As time passed, however, she relaxed; it was a caring touch, rather than an invitation to intimacy.

The tension of the day finally melted away, and her muscles relaxed one at a time. She hadn't felt this mellow in years, perhaps never.

Giving her a rueful grin, Tony released her hand and stood. "It's time I got you home."

Carolyn clasped her hands to preserve the warmth of his touch. "What time is it?"

"A little after nine." He grabbed the basket handles and held out the other hand to help her rise. "Ready?"

She took it, then stood and walked to the car, fingers entwined with his. It felt too right. Too good. Too . . . She refused to think any further.

She had just enjoyed a light dinner with a friend. Her emotional low was only because she'd enjoyed the novelty of having company and was reluctant to have the evening end. It was a pleasant change. Soon he'd be gone and she would revert to her old schedule. . . .

"We'll be home in time for the news. May I come in and watch it? I missed the six o'clock, since I was getting our dinner ready."

Her spirits rose immediately. "Sure. I'll make some coffee."

"I'd like that." Letting go of her hand, Tony opened her door, put the basket into the back seat, then got into the car. Before turning the key in the ignition, he stared at her; she felt his gaze searching her eyes, her cheeks, her slightly parted mouth. "You need to relax more often. It does wonders for your smile."

"Thank you—I think," she said dryly.

One corner of his mouth turned up sexily. "It also does wonders for your sense of humor."

She felt a little affronted at the suggestion. "What do you mean?"

"You have one, but when you're busy, you seem to put the fun part of you aside until you have time to use it."

She watched his mouth move, barely hearing the words. Their closeness inside the car, combined with the darkness outside, seemed to be casting a spell. She fought against the enchantment. "That's not true."

"And you don't always have free time."

"That isn't true, either."

Tony didn't reply. Instead, he moved his head slowly, inch by inch toward hers. Their breathing mingled. His blue gaze had turned lightning gray, and he looked at her so intently, she worried that her soul might be exposed.

"Tony."

"Yes?"

"Just . . . Tony."

His lips lightly brushed hers from one side to the other. She arched her neck to maintain the light contact. But he pulled away. He looked at her again. This time his eyes narrowed into slits, their gaze piercing. Once more he grazed her mouth with the caress of a butterfly's wing. His warm breath touched her face, her cheeks, and then moved down her neck. She leaned forward.

"Please," she murmured, asking for the teasing to stop.

A low moan echoed in his throat and his mouth covered hers; still moving slowly, still gentle, very restrained. But firm. Her breath caught in her throat. She wanted more. She *ached* for more.

But she couldn't ask him.

Tony's arms came around her with infinite slowness and pulled her against the strength of his chest. Now her hands rested on his broad shoulders, wanting to hold tight, to feel his firmness against all of herself. Instead, she lay against him, frightened by the rising tide of emotion that threatened to swamp her.

She wanted him to sweep her off her feet.

She wanted him to leave her alone.

Her intense need finally overcame her fear. Slowly she let her arms creep around his neck and pull him closer, deepening the kiss.

But Tony pulled away, briefly resting his forehead on hers; he took a deep breath. "Let's go home." His voice rasped down her spine.

Carolyn nodded, remaining silent. Her heart beat erratically at the thought of making love to Tony again. As the car sped toward her house she worried. If she let Tony close, let him break the defenses she'd so carefully built, he'd demand even more from her. Finally she spoke, putting a tiny hint of defiance into her tone. "I . . . we—maybe we shouldn't do anything."

Tony moved the car into the passing lane. "Like what?"

"Like making love," she said. She felt a blush tinge her cheeks and was grateful for the darkness.

"Okay."

"I mean it, Tony."

He pulled around another car and went smoothly into the right-hand lane. "Okay."

At his agreement Carolyn felt both secure and depressed. Would she always be this uncertain around Tony, or would it disappear over time? She wasn't sure she wanted to wait around to find out.

The ride home went much too quickly and they were pulling into Carolyn's driveway before she'd figured out a way to stay in control.

Common sense told her what to do: say good-night and let him go home. But her heart won the day. "Would you still like to see the news?"

He turned toward her, eyes gleaming, and said, "I'd love to."

Once inside, she made coffee, too aware of Tony leaning in the doorway, watching her every move. Unwilling to look at him again, Carolyn placed mugs upon the counter and stared at the pot as if she could will it to hurry up and finish.

"Why are you so nervous?" Tony's voice was low, but his challenge was unmistakable. "I don't make you react that way, do I?"

"I'm not nervous."

She sensed that he'd come up behind her, but still refused to turn around. When his arms slipped around her waist and pulled her gently against his own hard form, she instantly responded to the warmth of his body. Her breath caught in her throat. "Talk to me," he said in a low voice. "Tell me what's going on in your head."

"Nothing," she whispered. "You're imagining things."

"You're afraid of something," he insisted quietly. "Is it me?"

How could she put her feelings into words? She simply felt vulnerable with him. Her emotions were too close to the surface; all she wanted was to turn in his arms and lay her head upon his chest. She craved the safety and security he offered; it was something she hadn't felt in a long time. A very long time.

Instead, eyes closed, she allowed herself to relax against him. But she remained silent.

"Relax," he whispered into her ear. "I promise I won't bite."

"So you say *now*," she finally managed.

"I won't. Whatever your imagination is working overtime on, it has nothing to do with me." He gave a warm chuckle and the sound vibrated down her spine and into her very core. "Unless you're dreaming about me making love to you, inch by delicious inch. In that case, you may have cause for worry."

"Why?"

He crossed his hands in front of her, resting each palm just under her breasts. His thumbs flicked petal lightly against her nipples. "Because if that's what you fear, it's my fear, too. Only your fear might be that I want to make love to you, and my fear is that I won't get the chance."

She wouldn't ask. She didn't want to know. But logic had little to do with what she was feeling right now. "Is that really your fear?"

He placed a lingering kiss upon the soft spot just below one ear. "After spending the night in Corpus

Christi, making love as if we had known each other for a hundred years, my biggest worry has been that I'd never get the chance again. It was too good to throw away, Carolyn."

"There's more to me than making love."

"I know. Friendship is just as important as any other facet of a relationship. But making love is important, too."

"You don't have to make love to be friends." Her voice was a mere whisper, a token of resistance. Somewhere deep inside her a warning sounded. If she kept him talking, she might not succumb to her own, clamoring desires....

"There's a bigger commitment at stake when you decide to be more than friends. And when that happens, the missing part is the one that's important."

"Like now?"

"Like now," he repeated. "We're already friends. We've already been lovers. If we continue to be together, we need to be both."

She stiffened. "Is this a threat?"

"How could it be a threat?"

"Are you saying that if I don't go to bed with you, you won't see me anymore?"

His palms covered her breasts now, supporting their weight. "Don't you care about our relationship? You know I wouldn't threaten you."

He waited. Her silence was her answer.

A low chuckle came from him. "Okay, Carolyn. You've answered. I'm not sure I understand why you can't say the words, but if that's the way you want it, I'll go along."

Still she was silent. Damn the man! He'd understood that she couldn't make a verbal commitment, any more than she could deny that she cared!

His hands left her breasts and she felt bereft, until he slowly turned her to face him. His mouth came down in a gentle kiss that promised more—much more—to follow. Tension, ever present between them, ignited, and she curled her arms around his neck and held him tightly. She didn't want him to go and leave her alone tonight. She wanted to make love with him, to show him what she felt.

Tony pulled away, his breathing ragged. "To hell with coffee," he murmured, his mouth seeking other pleasure points, other sensitive areas that demanded his attention.

But it wasn't enough. Just as she had done three months ago, Carolyn took the lead. Holding his hand, she walked with him down the darkened hall to her bedroom.

The room was barely illuminated by the pool lights that shimmered through the green water outside; they cast an eerie, wavering reflection onto the wall and ceiling above the bed. Standing in front of the big window, Carolyn stripped off her suit and blouse, then stood still, wearing only a transparent, peach-colored bra and minuscule, matching slip.

"Such sexy underthings to wear and not have anyone see," he said huskily, sliding a finger under one bra strap and easing it over her shoulder. Her skin was soft and creamy as ever. "What a shame."

"You're seeing them," she answered, taking courage from the admiration she saw shining in his eyes. "Am I the only one getting undressed?" She'd repeated her own words, without prodding this time, highlighting the memories of their first night together.

Tony's low laugh set her spirits dancing. He shed his clothing quickly, then stood in front of her, a magnificent, naked male. Carolyn wondered what she'd done to deserve such beauty.

She reached behind him with a hand that shook slightly and tugged at the leather thong that held his ponytail. When his hair fell loose, it resembled a mane, all sun-streaked and flowing. He was too handsome for words.

"Be with me," she murmured. "Be a part of me."

His hands touched her slim waist, bringing her closer. "I am."

Tony held her to him with hands and mouth and rigid body, and she reveled in the touch, the scent, the sight of him. She rested her hands on his shoulders and saw their whiteness stand out plainly against his tanned skin.

The light from the pool played across their bodies, moving, teasing, hiding. Carolyn pulled back and looked up, inwardly melting at the sight of the softness in his eyes. She traced a thick, dark brow with her fingertip, trailing it down his cheek and along his jaw, then moving to the hollow in his throat.

"You're very special."

"So are you, darlin'. So are you." The huskily spoken endearment touched her somewhere deep inside and reignited more fires that had long been banked.

"I'm scared," she finally admitted. *Of you*, she added to herself.

His arms tightened around her for a moment, then were still. He took a deep breath and brushed a kiss onto her parted lips. "Tell me what wrongs to right or what dragons to fight, Carolyn, and I will. But I have to know what it is I'm fighting."

"You scare me."

He smiled, but there was a sadness in his eyes. "No, darlin'," he corrected gently. "*You* scare you. I'm just someone to focus on. You already know I'd never hurt you."

She heard what he said, but her gaze was trapped by his mouth. Craving had grown into overwhelming need. She wanted him so badly that she could taste the wanting, yet he was making no further moves. Was she to take the initiative here, too? She'd never done anything like this before and didn't know if she could handle it. It was one thing to lead him to her bedroom and tease him into stripping, quite another to initiate making love.

She must have shown him what she was thinking, for she saw his smile soften. This time he did the leading.

He reached down with a strong, graceful gesture and picked her up, holding her against his chest. She wrapped her arms around his neck as he walked to the side of the massive bed. In one, smooth motion, they sprawled across the cool, thick comforter, pillows falling everywhere around them. Tony tossed a few more onto the floor.

Carolyn stopped him. "Leave them. I don't care," she said, covering his mouth with her own as she lay across him, intertwining her smooth legs with his lightly furred ones. She felt her nipples pout when she pulled across the raspiness of his chest, but the deep, inner craving she'd felt since their first meeting was still present, waiting to be satisfied.

And Tony was the only one who could do that.

Dear, sweet, sexy Tony.

6

CAROLYN WOKE in a tangle of comforter, sheets and pillows. Best of all, she woke to the sight of Tony, sitting on the side of her bed. He held a freshly brewed cup of steaming coffee in his hand.

"Good morning, darlin'," he drawled in his low, sexy voice, and she could have sworn she heard a note of fun. "Have some coffee. I just made it."

She groaned and closed her eyes again, secretly savoring the sight, the experience, but unwilling to let him know just how much she enjoyed having him with her when she woke up. "What are you still doing here?"

"Waiting for you to wake up, so I can take you to work." His tone was laced with humor. She opened one eye, then the other, disgusted to see she was right. He was smiling!

"It's too early to smile. Besides, I can drive myself to work," she muttered grumpily, reaching for the cup he was holding.

"I've got reason to be happy." He didn't explain, letting the momentary silence speak for him. "Besides, your car is already at work. Remember?"

She'd forgotten that Tony had picked her up from the office last night. After the picnic they'd come home and made passionate, delicious and satisfying love. But he was still supposed to be gone by now. She wasn't supposed to get used to having him around. She didn't want that; it was too much like a steady relationship. Her biggest fear was of the pain she would suffer when the relationship was over.

Carolyn sat up and sipped at the coffee until daylight began to penetrate her brain. "I could have called a cab."

"And paid a king's ransom? Houston isn't a cab kinda town. Besides, does that sound like the behavior of a gentleman?"

She took another gulp of coffee, still happy that he was here and thankful that he was so sweet.

She yawned and stretched. "What time is it?"

"Eight o'clock." He took the cup from the nightstand, then got to his feet. "Hurry up, lazybones. I called your office and told them you'd be two hours late for work." He gave her a kiss on the nose and walked toward the door.

That got her attention, and her gaze darted to the clock. She'd overslept, by two hours! "Why didn't you wake me?" she exclaimed.

"Because you needed the extra sleep." He spoke over his shoulder and left the room.

She didn't have time to debate the subject. Carolyn jumped from bed and ran to the bathroom. Ten minutes later she'd showered and had applied a quick dash of makeup that she promised herself she would repair when she got to work. As she reached for her suit, Tony came in with another cup of coffee. She gave him a quick smile, took another gulp, then slipped into a suit skirt and flipped a blouse off its hanger.

Reaching for her jacket, Carolyn glanced again into the mirror. She checked her hem, the zipper and turned. "How do I look?"

"Great, as usual," Tony said, lounging on the bed. For a split second she wanted to throw her coat to the floor and join him. But sanity ruled now.

"You're blind," she said instead, trying to be flippant.

He went on as if she hadn't spoken. "But not half as beautiful as you looked last night. You made one hell of a spectacular image then. Pillows scattered all around you, golden hair mussed and your eyes gleaming with stars. You looked like a goddess. Or a slave in a sultan's tent, waiting to please her master."

She wanted to laugh at the fanciful picture he'd painted, but couldn't. Mike had never seen her in that light. It had taken Tony, sexy, wonderful Tony, to recognize that side of her. His perception was both fabu-

lous and frightening. Could he see more—perhaps traits
and secrets she didn't *want* him to know about?

Keeping her expression as calm as she could, Carolyn reached for her purse. "Ready?" she asked brightly.

Tony seemed to be moving deliberately slowly. He
rolled off the bed, followed her out of the room and into
the hallway. She checked the coffeepot to make sure it
was off, then waited for him at the front door.

Tony followed her lead without speaking, but she
had a feeling that he was going along with her for his
own reasons.

They drove the ten minutes to her office building.
Carolyn breathed a sigh of relief at having successfully
played the part of a sophisticate and turned to say
goodbye.

He finally spoke. "Dinner tonight. My house."

"I can't. I didn't do any work last night and I need to
catch up."

"You need vitamins and sleep," he retorted. "Tonight you'll start with dinner and a relaxing hour or so.
Then you can go home to your work."

She opened her mouth to protest, then closed it.
What harm could dinner do? She had to eat. Besides,
she'd have her car and leave whenever she wanted. "Are
you a good cook?"

He pulled into the circular driveway in front of her
office building. "Yes."

Confidence. No excuses, no explanations. Just "Yes."

She reached for the door handle. "I'll try to be there at seven."

"Carolyn." He said her name softly, firmly. But the feeling behind the word was what stopped her.

"Yes?"

Tony leaned over and kissed her gently on the mouth. It was a light kiss, but it held promise and hope and such a wonderful feeling of tenderness that it touched her deeply. "Take care."

A lump formed in her throat. No one had ever said those words to her with quite that meaning. The difference was that he cared.

"I will," she promised, smiling in return.

He drove off and she entered the building. The spot close to her heart, the spot that he had touched with his tender ways, stayed warm all day.

Jeff Harden entered her office late that afternoon and lounged in the wing chair across from her desk. "So how did Cindy's files look?"

The files lurked in the trunk of her car. "They look fine, so far."

"Good. Do you want to take over her accounts?"

"Jeff..." she began, trying to find a way around this. She already had too much to handle.

"I know, I know," he said with his boyish grin. "It's a lot to ask. But you're one of the best in this office,

Carolyn. Someday you'll realize just how much we need and depend on you here. There's more than just a job at stake. You know that." He hesitated a moment for effect, then frowned. "Of course, I could give this assignment to Bob True . . . if you think you can't handle it."

There it was again—the unspoken promise that she would become a partner. *If* she played her cards right. But if she didn't do as he asked, Bob would be next in line. She'd worked damn hard to get this close. . . . "Okay, you talked me into it."

Jeff nodded, clearly satisfied he'd done well. "Good. Let me know if you hit any snags." He stood and walked out the door.

"Of course." It was something to say. She knew if she went to him with *any* problem other than a question with a tax or Internal Revenue ruling, it would look bad on her record.

Sighing heavily, she picked up the next piece of mail. From the look of the pile the secretary had just brought in, she might be working on it alone until it was time to leave for dinner. But a small part of her was happily anticipating the evening. Only three more hours to go and she'd be with Tony. . . .

TONY GLANCED AT THE CLOCK on the mantel. Carolyn was late. Maybe she'd forgotten. No. Her life was too organized for her to forget.

He glanced at the clock again. Less than a minute had passed. Dinner was cooked and keeping warm in the oven. A tossed salad was in the refrigerator. The table was set. There was nothing left to do but wait. He crossed to the wet bar and poured Scotch over a few ice cubes, then tasted the liquor, feeling the cold liquid turn to heat as it wound its way down to his stomach. He took a deep breath and told himself to relax.

She wouldn't stand him up. If nothing else, she'd call from her car phone and make up some excuse for not coming.

She'd remember. He was sure of it.

He sat down in the maroon and green plaid, over-stuffed, Morris chair and propped his feet on the matching ottoman. He had a feeling that before he came to terms with this woman, he would have turned honing his patience into an art form. He might as well begin learning now.

Tony closed his eyes and imagined her as he'd seen her at her most vulnerable. She lay beneath him and he was inside her, moving slowly, easily, just enough to insure that what he wanted would happen. It did. Her eyes opened wide, stared at him in surprise, then closed again. A wondrous smile tilted her lips. Her arms, wrapped around his body, tightened as if she were afraid of floating away. She was the most beautiful woman he'd ever seen. He almost cried at the sight of her. And her response was open, true. *Real.* When they made love, all the guards were down. After their love-making, she wrapped herself in his arms and fell asleep.

He remembered the night she'd fallen asleep in his arms after he'd learned just how close she'd been to her sister. The wall she'd built to protect herself had also stopped Carolyn from healing. Finally, through her tears, she'd acknowledged the grief, the betrayal she'd felt when her sister had stolen her husband. Since that emotionally explosive night they'd talked on the phone, had dinner together, made love, but she'd never again referred to her feelings for her sister and ex-husband.

His original suspicions had been proven correct. Carolyn had learned from her family how to maintain distance in a relationship, how to deflect emotional blows by building walls that were practically insurmountable, and how to burrow inside herself when an outbreak other than anger threatened. Carolyn had learned her lessons well, and had been vulnerable only to her sister and brother. Following her sister's betrayal, she had burrowed even deeper into her self, using her work as her only source of comfort and accomplishment.

Now he, Tony, was paying the price for the suffering her parents, sister and her ex-husband had inflicted. She was using him as the scapegoat for them all. That needed to be changed, and her tears last night had told him that she was finally facing a few of her nightmares.

But the fact remained that she was still holding her grief inside; the guilt had to be growing.

Grief had once been his constant companion, too. When he'd been young and just married, everything had seemed possible. When his son was born, he'd been sure of it. Then, as his business had soared, taking him away from home more and more, he'd promised himself that he would spend more time with his family. But he hadn't.

When their son died, Tony had thrown himself completely into his work, so that he wouldn't have a single moment to think about the loss they had suffered. At night he'd been so exhausted that he'd gone to sleep immediately.

Four years later he'd lost his wife, too. And had had to face his guilt for not paying enough attention to those he loved. He hadn't been there when Betty needed him, hadn't told Betty when he needed her. Most of all, Tony had had to come to terms with his own life, find out what was missing and what he wanted from it.

Not sure at first what that was, Tony had concentrated on what he didn't want. He didn't want to spend his life working too hard. He didn't want to hide in the dark, afraid of the sunshine, afraid of life. And he wanted no more working to hide from life.

He had to laugh at himself now. Having made that momentous decision, he'd fallen in love with a woman who was doing exactly that—and for exactly the same reasons.

The doorbell rang and his anxiety level sank. When he opened the door, he was rewarded with her apologetic smile. "I'm sorry. I got tied up and couldn't get out of a meeting."

He shrugged, feeling relaxed again. "Now that you're here, it doesn't matter."

She stepped over the threshold and he watched her walk into the formal living area, saw her study the room, much as he had done in her home. He followed her gaze, seeing his home through her eyes. Whereas her house was casual, his was formal. A blend of traditional furniture antiques made his home look heavier, he reflected. The darker colors that had been used— gold, forest green and deep red—added to that illusion. It was the same throughout the house.

"Would you like a drink? Or are you hungry?"

She smiled again. "I'm starved. I forgot to eat today."

"Then let's eat right now," he proposed.

But her attention was still on the furniture. "It's lovely," she murmured, running a hand over a low, rosewood cabinet.

"Thanks. I had little to do with it. My wife decorated, and I never had the expertise or energy to change it. Except my study and the kitchen," he added.

"What about the kitchen?"

He turned and led her down the hall. "I had both rooms renovated two years ago. They're where I spend most of my time when I'm home."

The kitchen was decorated in pristine white and navy blue, with bright splashes of cherry-tomato red. He walked past the island cooking area to a built-in double oven and pulled out a casserole dish, placed it on top of a burner, then reached for the salad in the refrigerator, hidden behind sleek cabinet doors. Tony knew she was watching every move he made and deliberately kept his expression bland.

Placing the meal upon a round, glass-topped table in front of a huge fireplace at the other end of the room, he cocked an eyebrow at her. "Dinner is served."

She sat down in the chair he pulled out for her and surveyed the table. Cheery, tomato-red place mats and napkins brightened the clear glass plates. Even wine- and water glasses sat in the right spot. "I'm amazed that a man would pay such attention to detail."

"Which detail?" Tony asked as he set the dishes upon wooden trivets in the center of the table and took the seat opposite her. "The fact that I remembered cloth napkins, or that I can use serving pieces, instead of dishing food out of a saucepan?"

The edge to his voice made Carolyn aware that she'd hit a nerve. "I'm sorry. I didn't mean to insult you."

"You didn't," he said quietly. "You patronized me."

She bristled. "I didn't mean to do that, either."

"You're lumping me in with all the other men, telling me that none of us are capable of caring about different things or behaving differently." He handed her the salad bowl. "I'm human first, Carolyn, and male second. You're assuming I'm exactly like Mike."

She should have known he'd cut straight to the heart of the matter. "Only in the broadest sense, Tony. If I made you feel that way, I'm sorry." She grinned. "It's just that a few men spoil the fine reputation most men have for fidelity, honor and integrity."

"Slick politicians with silver tongues, for one," Tony commented dryly. "And I believe I just demonstrated that I'm not a member of that group."

He won her hearty laughter for that. She didn't know how he did it, but Tony had a way of first confronting her, then making her feel at ease about the debate.

She scooped up a helping of the casserole: spicy chicken with vegetables and pasta, all enclosed in a flaky, golden crust, and set it on her plate. It smelled as good as it looked. While Tony filled her glass with ruby-red wine, she dipped her fork into the succulent dish and took a bite. It was delicious.

"You're an excellent chef, too," she said, reaching for her wineglass. "Is there anything you can't do well?"

He cocked a brow in a wicked gesture. "Is that a roundabout admission that I'm a good lover?"

"Roundabout," she admitted, laughing again. "But that won't get you out of answering the question."

"Nothing I'll admit to. You'll have to find out for yourself."

"Do you cook anything else, or is this your specialty?"

"I have a whole file box of recipes. I was forced into learning when my wife was ill, and found that I enjoyed it. I still do, but it's hard to get enthusiastic when there's only one to cook for."

"I understand that," she said, suddenly feeling awkward.

It was hard to imagine Tony with anyone, and she found that she resented the idea of another woman being with him. Even his wife. She wondered if he felt the same way about Mike, but decided not to follow that train of thought. She didn't want any strings attached to this relationship, she reminded herself.

They kept the conversation light and savored the meal. By the time they were halfway through Carolyn was completely relaxed and enjoying their friendly debate.

After coffee and a delicious slice of cheesecake dripping with raspberry syrup, Carolyn reluctantly realized she should leave. She followed Tony into the living room and allowed herself to be persuaded to have a small glass of Frangelico. He sat down on the couch and patted the seat next to him. She took the hint.

"What is it you have to do that's so important?" Tony asked.

"Paperwork. It's lurking in my trunk, multiplying in the dark." She tried to make a joke of it, but they both knew she honestly felt that way.

"Why don't you bring it in and do it while I clean the kitchen?"

That sounded tempting. She didn't want the evening to end, but didn't see how she could work, knowing that he was so close by. She finally shook her head. "No. I need to spread it out at home. If I don't finish, I can leave the papers sorted and come back to them later."

His fingers played with a strand of hair that touched her neck. She wanted to curl up against him. Instead, she sat stiffly and stared into her drink.

"What about tomorrow night?" His tone was low, the question easy to ask. The effect was mesmerizing.

"What about it?"

"Dinner again?"

"More paperwork."

"Dinner at your house." His tone brooked no argument now. "I'll bring the food, you supply the kitchen. That way you can do your paperwork while I prepare dinner, and afterward I can watch TV while I pretend I'm not watching you."

She might as well be honest about it. "I'd love it." Then she stood, forcing herself to leave now, while she could. She had to be crazy to let this relationship go any further, yet she was doing precisely that. "I have to go," she told him, unwilling to be this close, knowing that the next step would have her falling into his arms. She wasn't ready for that again. Not yet, at any rate.

Tony stood, too, his stance still relaxed. "I'll walk you out."

Carolyn wished she understood herself. She wished she understood Tony. Why was he pursuing a cold woman like her? Nothing about this relationship made any sense.

At her car he smiled, gave her a gentle hug and told her to drive carefully.

Dejected, Carolyn stepped into her car, revved the engine and pulled out of the driveway. It wasn't until she was halfway home that she recalled that Tony's For Sale sign had had a Sold sign attached to it.

Tony Valentine had sold his house. That meant he was moving. Where was he going?

That thought depressed her even more. She was afraid of getting involved with him; she was even more afraid of *not* having him in her life.

The following days began to form a pattern. Carolyn worked until the office officially closed. She didn't stay longer to do her extra work. Instead, she shoved it into her briefcase to do at home. Half an hour after she reached her door, Tony arrived with groceries and started puttering in the kitchen, while she worked in her study.

She knew she was chicken, but she never asked him where he was planning to move to. And he never volunteered any information.

Occasionally she'd hear him on the phone with his financial advisor, giving instructions or getting input on buying, selling or seeking out stocks, puts and calls. More often she heard the soft clank of pots and pans and the slightly off-key humming of a song.

But the night always ended in her bed, whether they made love or just cuddled and fell asleep. Tony would leave in the early morning, an hour or two before she woke up to get ready for work.

Always, always, she knew he was in the house.

And she felt better, safer, happier, more contented at having him there. But she would never admit it. If she said the words aloud, he might disappear—and then she'd be all alone again.

Better not to tempt fate. When he'd gone—she was sure he would go, one day—she would not have to acknowledge the immense void he'd left behind.

They went out to dinner the night that Tony signed the papers on the house. He lifted his glass in a toast. "Here's a thank-you for the happiness I've shared with you over the last few months."

Smiling, she clinked her glass against his. But her fear that he was leaving had grown. It was time to broach the question. "Where will you move, now that the house has been sold?"

Tony shrugged. "I'm putting the furniture I want to keep in storage, then checking into the Casa Mañana Hotel for a month or so, until I decide what I want to do when I grow up."

They had never spoken of money, but Carolyn knew he had more than enough to live comfortably for the rest of his life. All the same, life was about more than money, and she was only beginning to realize how much more. "What do you think you want to do?"

His answer was almost instant. "Open a bed-and-breakfast place, with stables and hiking trails."

Her coffee cup stopped halfway to her mouth. "Are you serious?"

He nodded, and the twinkle in his beautiful, blue-gray eyes told her he knew his answer was a shock to her. "It's crazy, but that's what I want. I want the chance to do every day what I dreamed of doing on weekends, when I was so busy I could hardly find time to grab a cup of coffee."

"There can't be much money in those inns."

Tony shrugged again. "That wasn't the criterion. It would cover the bills, and I'd have time to enjoy life, meet new people, enjoy old friends, and cook. What more could I ask?"

"A little ambition?"

Tony's deep, husky chuckle set her body vibrating. "I don't have to worry about that, honey. You've got enough for both of us. Besides, I've already built a business and reaped the rewards of that hard work. That's the reason I can take things easy now."

A thought that had been playing at the back of her mind finally made its way to the fore. "Tony?" she asked tentatively. "Why don't you move into my place until you find what you want? After all, you're already there almost every evening."

Tony raised one brow in question. "Are you saying you like having me around?"

It took everything she had to form the next word, the one that would admit her feelings. She made it. "Yes."

His smile was slow in coming and warmed every part of her. "Careful, Carolyn," he teased. "That sounds like commitment—and you know how you feel about that. I accept."

"Tony," she warned, but knew her tone was light.

"And I promise to be the best roommate you ever had."

She finally laughed. "Since I've only had two in my lifetime, it won't be a hard record to break."

"See?" he retorted. "I'm ahead of the competition already!"

She didn't know what to say. But for the first time in a long time, things felt right.

7

CAROLYN'S newfound routine with Tony was disrupted by the sale of his house. He then began the tough job of sorting through the furniture, papers and personal memorabilia that had been cubbyholed in every attic, chest and closet over twenty years. He went to his home in the morning, as if to any ordinary job, worked all day, then returned to Carolyn's for dinner.

Before long it became clear that the sifting and sorting was emotionally draining. Carolyn soon knew when Tony was sorting through his son's belongings by the weary look in his eyes. Watching memories of another life, a life she knew nothing about, rip through him was the toughest thing she'd ever done. She had no idea how to combat the feelings he was reliving. She wasn't even sure she should try and decided on silent support instead.

In bed with him in the dark she held him closely until sleep overcame them both. But she still sensed that his dreams were filled with disturbing memories.

Wishing there was something she could do to ease his heartache, she tentatively offered to go through the boxes for him, if it would help. But he refused, and doggedly went on going to the house. And night after night he awakened in the dark, shaking, sweat dripping from his body, a scream caught somewhere in his throat.

His mood lightened when he began going through his wife's papers and journals. Again, his dreams were riddled with old memories. But those memories occasionally seemed to be happy. In sleep he'd wrap himself around her as if she were an anchor. By day he was still wrung out and distant.

Carolyn called him every afternoon, hoping it would help him refocus on the present. Occasionally, Jeff Harden would walk in on her conversation, but she didn't care. She wanted the Tony she knew back again—all the time, not just in the evening. By now she knew he would welcome her warmly when she got home, as if nothing unusual was happening.

Because her attention was focused on him now, she thought it would be easier for her to talk about his problem. But when Carolyn tried to get him to give her some answers, Tony brushed off her questions with a smile and a yawn. It was the first time he hadn't let his guard down before her, and it hurt deeply.

His implicit rejection brought her full circle—back to her own problems. Sensing Tony must feel just as isolated whenever she shut him out, she nonetheless believed that circumstances were different in her case. They were, weren't they? But the question refused to go away. Was she trying too hard to find an answer— or not hard enough?

Acknowledging her love for Tony would be the hardest thing Carolyn had ever done. That much she knew. Finally she did—if only to herself. Trying to maintain a semblance of calm she didn't feel, she told herself that everything ended: life, the seasons, relationships with friends and customers, and so would her time with Tony. She would enjoy what they had together before he found a woman who better fitted him and his life-style.

The two of them were not a good match. She knew that much, though she didn't want to acknowledge it. The differences were obvious: the way they looked at work and play, scheduled their lives, decided what was important and what was trivial. She was sure their similarities wouldn't be able to compensate for the differences, and that made her fatalistic about their affair.

All the same, the very idea of Tony falling in love with another woman hurt her so much that she had to hold her breath against the pain—a pain that kept returning like a bad dream, at odd times, both by night and day. Each time she had to force herself to suppress the pain.

These fluctuations were driving her crazy. It was as if she was condemned to spend a part of every day on an emotional seesaw. She missed him when he wasn't with her; she resented the times he *was* nearby and wanted her attention.

None of it made any sense. All of it was frustrating and draining. She'd never been indecisive before. Friends had often told her they thought she had an opinion on everything, and occasionally she'd been assured that was not intended as a compliment. With Tony, however, everything was upside down.

She didn't work late anymore. Each time she left the office and hurried toward her car, she resented the thought that Tony was waiting for her.

At the same time, she looked forward to finding him waiting for her. She loved walking into the house and being enveloped in a hug. She enjoyed their conversations about her day. She enjoyed sitting across from him at the dinner table and discussing whatever small emergency had created havoc with her normally highly organized day. His witty comments and occasionally acerbic sense of humor often turned what had seemed like an emergency into an anthill, rather than the insurmountable peak it had felt like earlier in the day.

She reveled in making love with Tony and sleeping with him, his hand lying possessively across her waist or lightly palming her breast. His warm breath on her back had the effect of a sensuous security blanket. Every night Carolyn simply curled up against him, smiled into the darkness and closed her eyes, falling asleep as if she hadn't a care in the world.

She adored waking up in the morning to a still-damp Tony, fresh from the shower. He'd kiss her, then hand her a cup of steaming coffee with just the proper amount of cream. The scent of toasting bagels filled the air. The taste of his lips was heaven. She even enjoyed leaving him in the house. Since he set off later than she did, it felt as if everything that had to do with daily living was in his capable hands.

ALL THIS TIME Tony had never said a word about the inner turmoil that she knew he had to be aware of by now. But every evening during dinner, he stared at her through narrowed eyes, as if waiting for her to say something.

Finally she did.

Broiled fish in a light tomato sauce had been cooked to perfection. Salad, tossed with a light, Greek dressing was the perfect complement. Although the meal was delicious, Carolyn was restless, pushing the food around her plate.

Tony put down his fork, leaned forward and stared at her. "Tell me, Carolyn," he urged firmly. "Tell me and let's talk about it."

"I think you need to find something to do. A new career. Something that will put focus back in your life."

"I have the realtor looking now. Occasionally I go with her," he answered.

"I mean something more like work. A regular job," she insisted. She was determined not to get into the little matter of Tony driving around with another female all day. That would be nothing more than a childish reaction, an acknowledgment of her own insecurity.

"A 'regular job'?" he asked dryly. "A job you can tell your friends about so you can finally talk about me, instead of never mentioning me at all?"

"There's nothing wrong with having a career," she declared defensively. "Even millionaires work."

"And so do I. I spend more time on the phone with brokers than you do with clients."

"You know what I mean."

Tony sat back. "Why is it so important that I have something to do?" His blue-gray gaze was sharp. "Are you afraid that I'll focus on you?"

"No." That was a lie, and she knew it.

"Really." That was a statement, not a question. "Now why don't I believe you?"

Carolyn lifted her chin. "You need something that will keep your mind occupied."

"Why are you so worried? Why does it have to be a career? I have enough money to last me comfortably for the rest of my days. I don't need help, either in paying bills or financing a project."

"I'm not worried, but everyone needs a purpose." She tried not to let him hear the panic she was feeling. "When there's something to do, it keeps the mind active and the body in shape. Don't you think so?"

Taking his time, Tony sipped at his chilled white wine.

Carolyn suddenly felt as if she'd been struck by a thunderbolt. At last she understood why she needed to have Tony busy. If Tony was as preoccupied with a career as she was, he wouldn't have time to notice her compulsive behavior. Then he wouldn't find out she couldn't commit herself to a relationship, that she was unworthy of being loved.

There would be no threat of exposure as a less-than-perfect person.

Tony's voice burst into her thoughts. "I think you want me to work so you won't have to worry about me. Believe me, I'm fine now."

He was wrong, and that took some of the pressure off. "That's not true. You walk in the door every evening and I can see there's sadness in your eyes."

"Of course there is. I'm learning to accept it." He stared at her as if he could read her mind. "What are *you* sad about, Carolyn?"

The doorbell rang and she sighed with relief. It didn't matter who was on the other side of the door; she'd been saved from another dose of Tony's intense scrutiny.

The look of satisfaction on her brother's grinning face told her he was pleased by her surprise. "Never thought you'd see your brother without a formal invitation, did you?"

Happy laughter bubbled up, and Carolyn opened the door wider to give him a big hug. "Never thought I'd see you without your better half, either." She pulled back from their embrace. "Where's Tammy? Are the parents okay?"

He nodded, answering the last question first. "The folks are just the same as always," he told her reassuringly. "And my better half, as you put it, is at a teachers' conference in San Antonio. A sitter's watching the kids until I get home, so I decided to make use of the poor girl to surprise you."

Carolyn gave him another quick hug, happy to see him again. After all, they had once been very close. "I'm glad. I've missed you so much."

He stared at her, love in his eyes. "Your phone calls are too brief. Especially since Cora's death."

A pang arrowed its way through her heart, but she managed a quick smile and gave his shoulder a squeeze.

"I'm fine. Really." She was surprised to find the words were true. "I really am."

"Sure. . . ." he drawled disbelievingly, but she knew he was still worried.

"Honest!" She raised her hand in the air as if taking an oath.

Ed smiled at the gesture. Then something distracted him and he glanced over her shoulder. Without turning, she knew Tony must be standing behind her. She hadn't yet told Ed anything about him.

Turning now, she slid one arm around her brother's waist and gently prodded him toward Tony. "Ed, I'd like you to meet Tony Valentine. Tony, this is my big brother Ed."

Tony shook the younger man's hand. "Good to meet you. Your sister is rather closemouthed when it comes to her relatives."

"You didn't know she had a brother?"

"I knew she had one. She just forgot to mention that you also lived in Houston."

Carolyn watched each take measure of the other. Wary, they both seemed unwilling to draw conclusions just yet. But she knew that Tony had sensed her closeness with her brother and that Ed had raised an eyebrow, both at the sight of Tony's ponytail . . . and the impression that Tony gave, of being as relaxed in her home as she was.

"Have you known Carolyn long?" Ed asked.

"Several months," Tony answered easily. "I met her around the time your sister died."

Ed nodded thoughtfully. "Before or after?"

Carolyn was about to interrupt, but felt Ed's arm tighten around her waist. "During," Tony answered.

Ed's gaze narrowed even more, but Tony didn't seem intimidated. Instead he played the host. "I just opened a new bottle of wine. Would you like to join us?"

"I'd like that."

They went into the dining room and sat down. Ed took pains to show her he'd noticed the half-eaten dinner, but didn't comment. Tony reached inside the cabinet and pulled out another wineglass, then served him.

Ed raised his glass. "To my sister's success and happiness."

Tony raised his and smiled at her sexily, making her cheeks grow warm. "To outrageous deeds and fun-loving times."

Ed's brows rose again in question—after all, it was an odd statement—but he drank.

Both men set their glasses on the table and stared challengingly at each other.

Carolyn felt her own ire rising. Two grown men were readying for a fight, acting as if she were the prize. "How are the children?" she asked brightly, hoping to capture her brother's attention.

"Just fine. How's your job?"

"Just fine," she retorted dryly.

Ed nodded. He didn't seem to realize she'd just given him a repeat of his own answer. He watched Tony take another mouthful of fish.

"Pass the salt, will you, Ed?" Tony asked casually.

Ed placed the shaker in front of Tony's plate with a light, snapping sound. "My sister must think a lot of you. She's not used to cooking. For anyone. I asked her to contribute to Thanksgiving dinner one year and she brought a bowl of something or other she'd bought from a restaurant."

Tony shook the salt over his fish, though Carolyn was sure the action was more for show than anything else. "She's still not used to it. I did the cooking."

Ed's brows rose yet again. "And brought it here?"

Carolyn heaved a sigh. It was time to step in and stop the slaughter before it began. Besides, Tony would win and she didn't want Ed's blood all over the carpeting. "Tony lives here, Ed."

Her brother's shock was not feigned. "Lives here?"

Carolyn nodded.

"In this house? Your house?"

Carolyn nodded again.

Ed leaned back, his expression still reflecting shock. "Well, I'll be damned."

Tony took another mouthful of his fish, obviously relishing her brother's response to the news. Carolyn didn't know which man she most wanted to kick. If Tony had his way, the whole world would know about their relationship. Indeed, he seemed to believe everyone should know they were a couple. She wasn't ready for that.

All the same, Ed deserved a dressing-down; he was acting as if he were her father, instead of a brother who had, in fact, already complained that she wasn't in a relationship, soon after her divorce.

Ed gave Carolyn a hard stare. "Carolyn, would you mind if we spoke privately?"

She should have known a confrontation was coming. Sighing wearily, she stood and led Ed into her bedroom. Only when they reached the room she now shared with Tony did it dawn on her that if anything of his was lying around, it would only serve to inflame Ed's temper still more. But it was too late to turn back.

Once they reached the middle of the room, Carolyn confronted her brother, keeping her fingers crossed. She was afraid to look around her, so she didn't. "Whatever is on your mind, Ed, say it now and let me get back to my dinner. I'm tired and don't feel like arguing."

"Oh, yeah? But you do feel like living with some ponytailed guy who cooks for you while you support him? Didn't you learn your lesson with a ne'er-do-well like Mike? Do you remember Mike at all?" His gaze narrowed. "Does this guy drink like Mike used to?"

"Yes, yes, yes, and no."

"Are you crazy?" he cried.

"Yes."

Ed sighed, his frustration so apparent and brotherly concern so real that she almost took pity on him. But not quite. "I don't remember having any input into your choice of a marriage partner, brother."

His expression grew incredulous. "You're not thinking of marrying this guy, are you?"

"No." She shook her head, surprised how easily the answer had come. "But it's *my* right to choose who I spend my private time with, Ed. Not yours."

She heard another sigh, but this one sounded more like defeat. "Is he nice, or does he just cook a good meal?"

She slipped her arms around her brother's waist and gave it a squeeze. "Both. And a good wife is hard to find."

"Don't get smart, Carolyn." Ed's arms encircled her now and hugged back. "I've got sense enough to know a predator when he's in front of me. That man is as dangerous as a hungry shark."

She looked up. "Think so?"

He nodded. "Definitely. Don't let him hurt you, Carolyn. You deserve more. You deserve the best."

"I'll keep that in mind."

"You might keep it in mind, but half the time you don't believe you deserve anything good."

"That's not true."

"Yes, it is," he persisted. "You've always thrown the good stuff away, thinking that if you didn't work for it, it wasn't worth keeping. It's as if you don't think you deserve good things to happen to you."

"Ed..." she began, but couldn't deny the truth of his words. What he said might well be true. At least, it had been true enough of her past behavior to give him reason to worry today. But she'd changed, without even realizing it. "That used to be true," she began.

"Don't tell me differently, Carolyn. That was always the biggest difference between you and Cora. She figured out what she needed to feel good, then found it and hung on. She often said she deserved the best."

Carolyn's breath caught in her throat. He was right. Cora had always known what she wanted. She might have looked frail, even retiring, but she'd gone after exactly what she wanted—and usually gotten it.

Carolyn knew she was dedicated, too, but wasn't so sure what she wanted or deserved. In relationships she'd settled for too little. That was what had set her apart from Cora, and Ed clearly knew it.

"Are you reminding me that Cora isn't here to go after Tony?"

Ed's expression grew stubborn. "I'm reminding you that Tony is the kinda guy who knows what he wants. You still haven't got a clue about what you're after."

She bit her tongue, but had to ask. "Are you saying that Cora would have gone after him?"

Large hands pressed into her shoulders. "Dammit, Carolyn! You're not listening! Whether she would have gone after Tony or not isn't the question! I don't give a damn about the man out there, except whether he's going to help or hurt you!"

"It sounds to me like you think I don't know the difference!"

"Your track record hasn't been that good in the past." Ed's words stung like salt on a wound, making tears film her eyes. Ed's sigh was as heavy as his hands were light. "Ahh, Carolyn, don't cry," he said softly. "I didn't mean it. Honest."

Plump tears rolled down her cheeks, but she refused to wipe them away, preferring to look her brother straight in the eye. "Yes, you did, Ed. It's too late to back down now. You think I don't know what I want. You're wrong. If that were the case, I wouldn't have made it this far." She gestured toward the room around them, then pointed to the pool, gleaming eerily in the moonlight. "I wouldn't be able to afford all this."

"It's your personal life I was talking about."

He'd struck home again. "*I* control who lives here and who doesn't! *I* control who will be in my life and who won't!"

"Fine," he said softly. "I'll take your word for it."

"And Tony is part of it—for now."

"Look, all I was saying was that he's nothing like..." Ed stopped, probably not wanting to complete the sentence and risk bringing on more tears, she thought.

Carolyn tilted her chin in the air. "Like Mike? I already know that. According to your own opinion of Mike, Tony has nowhere to go but up."

"At the risk of repeating myself, he's a lot more dangerous than Mike ever was. He'll never give you the babies you always wanted. He's not the type."

She almost doubled at that blow. That was the one topic that was taboo. She'd always wanted babies, four or five of them. And she would raise them very differently from the way she and her siblings had been raised. Ed knew that.

Carolyn swallowed hard, and the tears spilled over. "That's below the belt."

"I know it," Ed said defensively. "But can't you see that if that's what you want, you'll never get it from him? You're not going after what you want. You're settling, Carolyn. When we were kids, we promised we'd all have the best."

She sighed. "And when you become an adult, you realize that those childish dreams were just that—childish."

"Tammy proved to me that they were real, honey. You, Cora and I were right when we dreamed. Dreams can come true. They did for me." He tilted her chin toward himself. "And however much you don't want to admit it, Cora and Mike were happy."

"I helped her at every turn, Ed. She was my family, my best friend. I'd have given her anything. But I didn't plan on her taking my husband."

"He was never really yours. You two never fitted together. Not really."

Unwilling to discuss her ex-husband any further, Carolyn smiled weakly. She knew it was forced, but saw that Ed looked relieved. "Now, come have dessert with us. Maybe you'll see another side to Tony, one you can get along with."

"I'll have dessert, but don't expect me to like the guy. He's already admitted to being outrageous."

"I labeled him that."

"At least you had the common sense to see it," her brother commented. "And that's all I'm going to say. I promise to try and behave myself, as long as he does the same."

"I'll settle for that," she said, leading the way out of the room, but she knew Ed would never see Tony as anything but dangerous.

How could he, when she knew Tony was just that?

8

HE'LL BE LEAVING SOON. She'd spoken those words with such confidence. So much false bravado.

Carolyn stared at the stars glistening over her bed. Once again she was replaying the conversation she'd had with her brother. Knowing Ed loved her and was worried about her made his caring all the harder to take. He knew how much she had suffered for love already and just didn't want to see her hurt again. Neither did she.

Tony was asleep next to her, one hand resting on her abdomen, as if claiming and comforting, even in sleep. She loved the feel of his hand on her. She loved the feeling of being next to him in the dark. She loved all the feelings he produced in her.

And while loving him, she had to admit she had never been this frightened before.

Early in this relationship she'd promised herself that if she could keep her distance, she'd have it made. But she hadn't been able to keep herself from loving Tony.

And she wanted none of this loving. Yet every time she thought of losing him, panic set in. She prayed he wouldn't see her flaws. That he'd miss her inadequacies. Tossing and turning, she worried. Not until dawn peeped through the windows and found her curled securely against Tony's body did she truly fall asleep.

CAROLYN'S BREATH flowed seductively over Tony's chest like warm water. He held her close, aware once again that she only showed her need of him in sleep. When she was awake, she pretended that she could do without him. But he knew better.

For whatever reason, Carolyn was petrified of getting close to someone. No, not just "someone;" he'd seen that she was close to her brother. She was afraid of getting close to him, Tony Valentine—maybe to any man who overstepped the boundaries she set. He didn't know any more.

She sighed and snuggled closer. Tony tightened his embrace and she settled against him once more.

A fierce feeling of possessiveness washed over him, making him more determined than ever to break down those barriers.

He had to make her admit how good they were together. Why was she so damn stubborn, refusing to acknowledge the truth? Most people didn't have what they did, but struggled along with the business of living together, anyway. Carolyn and he had a relationship that others would kill for, yet she didn't seem to care if it lasted. Damn!

There had to be a way to get through to her. Tony feared that if he didn't find it soon, he'd lose her. He couldn't stand the pain of losing someone he loved again.

DRIVING CAROLYN TO WORK was one of the bright spots for Tony, and he did it about three times a week. During that time, neither one had to answer a phone, cook or do any other menial job. They could talk and not feel guilty about taking the time from some necessary chore.

Tony enjoyed picking her up from work for the same reason. By late evening, Carolyn was tired, less resistant. She inadvertently allowed him to see the part of her that otherwise only showed when she snuggled up to him in bed. That part exposed the tough, working woman for what she was—vulnerable, afraid and alone. When night fell she became all woman, soft and sweet, willing to give as well as to receive.

He'd been so damn restless lately that the unsettled feeling almost overshadowed his enjoyment of being with Carolyn. Active all his life, Tony had usually had too much to do. But he'd put his life on hold for the past four months, so it was his fault he was so unsettled now. He'd put himself in this position and hadn't known what to do about it. Until recently.

Last week he'd finally started setting lunch dates with old friends and business associates. At first he'd been reluctant to take time away from his evenings with Carolyn, but had finally realized that their evenings were becoming strained. Perhaps Carolyn felt she had to work, in order to prove to him just how valuable she was. She didn't feel that their relationship needed work, because it—Tony—was always waiting for her, ready whenever she dropped her work for a while.

He was feeling more and more like a cross between a trained lapdog and a gourmet chef.

Yesterday's lunch date, Clive Walker, had suggested a new—temporary—job, something to keep his mind occupied and a grin on his face.

Clive had opened a new night spot on Westheimer and needed help training the staff. Tony had quickly agreed to oversee the bar a couple of nights a week for the next three weeks or so, while Clive got things under control. After all, Tony was looking at property two or three times a week, but that was all he had to do, and doing something—anything—was better than nothing. Besides, he hadn't tended bar since his college days, when he'd worked his way through school—and several girlfriends—by mixing drinks two or three nights a week. It had been great fun then. Perhaps it would be again.

Even Carolyn had tried to get him interested in work again, he reflected. And he did need something to occupy his time, his mind, while Carolyn was at work.

He found himself thinking of her all day, then worrying about her health all night. It wasn't doing either of them any good.

So, while his real estate agent looked for the perfect bed-and-breakfast place for him to redo, he might as well occupy his time by helping out a friend for fun and give Carolyn some breathing room.

Who knows? She might even miss him.

Who was he kidding? He was praying she'd miss him!

TUDY'S RESTAURANT, in the heart of the Galleria district, hummed with quiet, dignified activity. Wealthy Houstonians sat around well-appointed tables and discussed everything from politics to who was doing what with whom—all of which included politics.

Carolyn sat across from Tony, her smile warming his insides, her easy laughter lightening his heart.

"Did I mention how nice it is to be out with you?" she asked.

"No. And I can hear it as many times as you can say it."

Carolyn leaned forward, her hand lightly covering his. "I love being out with you."

"If I'd known you'd respond this way, I'd have taken you out more often. But most of the time you look so damn exhausted, I'm afraid to take you out, in case you fall asleep and plop your head in the soup." He was half teasing, half serious.

She knew it and felt chagrined; he was right. "I haven't been the best of company, have I?"

"Not since your brother came to visit. Since then, you've been working even harder and keeping your distance."

"That's not true." They both knew the words were false. Carolyn couldn't quite look him in the eye.

"Yes, it is. And it brought home something that I'd forgotten."

"What?"

"You've lived alone for a long time. In fact, there are times I think you need your own space, and it's hard to get when I'm around."

"You've been more than considerate."

"Well, I've come up with a temporary solution."

Carolyn's chocolate-brown eyes widened, and he was glad to see a touch of dismay there. "What kind of solution?"

"A business associate just started a new fifties club and needs some help, overseeing the bar area. Since I used to be a bartender, I'm going to help him out for a while."

Dismay grew into disbelief. "A club? You're going to work as a bartender in a club?"

That wasn't the most accurate job description, but it was close enough. He nodded, taking a mouthful of his rack of lamb. "Yes."

Carolyn carefully placed her fork on the side of her plate. "You've got to be kidding."

"No." He raised his brows. "Why would I?"

"You're actually going to tend bar?"

The tension in her voice put him on the alert. He placed his fork upon his plate. "Okay, Carolyn. What's on your mind?"

"I can't believe you're going to be a bartender! Is it the money? Have you lost investments? Do you need financial help? Have you got a problem I don't know about?"

"Don't be bashful, Carolyn," Tony said dryly; he finally saw where the conversation was leading. "Say what's on your mind."

"I thought I was." Her voice was as chilly, as distant as it had ever been. "And I think I deserve an explanation."

He raised one brow. "An explanation of what? My financial stability? My bartending ability? My friends?" He paused for a moment. "Or whether or not I should tell you of every decision I make, while you go through life, determined to remain independent, never to ask for advice."

"That's unfair, Tony. I'm talking about you, and you're trying to turn the tables and pretend this whole thing is my fault."

Tony sighed. "There is no 'fault,' Carolyn. A friend needed help and I offered my services."

"Do you think this is a way to keep up a corporate image? What if you want to begin a company later, and some investor remembers he saw you tending bar. That's not what a CEO puts on his résumé."

Tony whistled. "So that's what this is about. Your being upset has nothing to do with me not consulting you, but with my status in society—what you consider status."

"That's unfair."

"It's the truth." He knew he spoke harshly. "You're a snob."

The waiter checked with them about bread and wine, and Tony allowed Carolyn time to chew on his words while he stared at her in silence. He could feel her discomfort, but refused to back down until he'd found out exactly what was on her mind. She ran from personal conflict too often. But not this time.

"Tell me where I'm wrong. I can't read your mind."

Carolyn frowned. "Tony," she finally managed. "Please don't take a job like that. You're capable of so much more, used to so much more. It doesn't make sense that you should lower your standards like that."

Tony stroked the stem of his wineglass. "Is that really what you think? This has to do with standards?"

She nodded, and he wondered how someone so beautiful and even more intelligent could be so hooked on "status."

"Carolyn, I can't understand your problem. You know me well enough to realize that I'm going crazy doing nothing while I'm waiting for the real estate brokers to come up with the right piece of property for me. A friend needs help. I'm helping."

"I know, but—"

"And you work almost every night on paperwork that you don't have time to do during your already very long day."

"I know, but—"

"Besides, on those nights that I'm working for Clive, I'll be home just about the time you're climbing into bed."

"Tony, please don't do this." Carolyn leaned forward, all earnestness. "Please."

"Why?"

She opened her mouth, but no more words came out.

"Is it because you'll be embarrassed to be seen with a bartender?" he asked softly.

Her gaze darted around the room; it was panic. She didn't need to speak. He saw the answer.

Leaning back, Tony felt an unbelievable sadness. "So this has to do with what everyone thinks, instead of what you feel."

"That's not true." The protest was hollow.

Sighing heavily, Tony raised his knife and fork and attacked his rack of lamb. He might not feel hungry, but he'd be damned if he'd let her know just how despondent he was. Besides, he'd been thinking of this for several days. Carolyn had just heard of his plans in the past ten minutes. Maybe, after a little more time to digest the information, she would come around to his way of thinking.

It was worth a thought. He just wished he felt better about the odds being in his favor.

Later that night, Tony held Carolyn in his arms as she curled against him in sleep. They had gone to bed shortly after arriving home. Little had been said since they had left the restaurant. It was as if they had called a tentative truce.

He hoped her unreasonable attitude wouldn't last long, but realized sadly that everything between them had changed. The relationship had shifted into another gear, and he didn't know if it would be able to handle the changes. For all Carolyn's savvy in business and her intelligence in personal areas, she was not adaptable.

So, what makes you think she won't kick you out on your butt, Valentine? Tony's heart sank; he knew she would. Oh, maybe not right away, but sooner or later she would get scared again, look at her life and blame him for whatever unhappiness she felt. After all, it was easier to blame him than to change herself. And this time he couldn't bend.

If he had made a big enough dent in her heart, he might be able to salvage their relationship. If he didn't . . . Well, he'd just have to wait and see.

This issue was too big to ignore. It was time Carolyn faced her fears and learned to compromise; if she didn't, he would have to pull out.

He wasn't going to lose himself, just for the sake of being a small part of her life. The price was too high. The idea of not being with her was the hardest thing he'd ever imagined. But the thought of not being able to have even partial control of his own life was even worse. If only she would realize what she was doing to them both.

The next morning Carolyn awoke to find Tony's mouth lightly nuzzling her breast. In a lethargic mood, she moaned softly to let him know she was awake and enjoying his attention. He trailed kisses between her breasts and then favored the other breast, taking his time to stoke her desire. One hand traced a line, moving from breast to hip to inner thigh, where he stroked soft flesh. He stayed away from the spot that needed more attention.

Her mind still slightly fuzzy, Carolyn moved toward him. She had to assuage the need he was building from spark to fire. Instinct told her he was going to take his time, but she wanted results. Now.

A low chuckle vibrated against her breast. "I love it when you grow impatient, darlin'. I love it, because it tells me to slow down."

"No fair," she murmured, her voice sounding faint, even in her own ears.

"You got that right. And I won't hurry. It's my time, Carolyn, and I want what I want."

"Bastard."

"You're still not getting anything any faster than whatever I decide the pace is." His mouth marked a trail from breast to breast, then down to her navel to linger in a warm, wet kiss.

Carolyn moaned again, curling her fingers in his sandy-dark hair. This time his laugh reverberated against her abdomen, sending a shiver down her spine; she became aware of just how much he was willing to torture her before bringing relief.

His lips moved farther south and she held her breath, unsure whether to stop him or allow him to continue. The choice was taken out of her hands. The touch of his mouth, moist and warm, was so erotic, her head spun from the sensation. He knew where, how, when to touch to pull the response he wanted from her. And that was what he did.

Slowly. Patiently. Softly. Successfully.

Her fingers loosened their hold on him and clung to the spun percale bed sheets, as if anchoring her to the present. But it didn't work. Tony's mouth went on sensitizing her to nothing but himself. They were wrapped in a cloud of touch and imagination, losing sight of everything else that might have happened.

"Tony," she pleaded, begging him to end his torture.

"No," was his answer.

"But..."

"No, baby," he said softly, as if explaining to a simple child. "Relax. We have plenty of time. All the time in the world." He stroked her wet, slick skin. "You'll get there. I promise."

Then, as if to prove his point, he once more began the process of making love to her. Once more his mouth covered her, his hands tempting, teasing her breasts.

The beauty of her feelings made Carolyn want to cry. She wanted to rail at the frustrations that filled her, wanted to pretend his teasing wasn't taking her to the end of her rope. But she knew better.

Suddenly he brought her to the brink. She clung to the bed, her thoughts tumbling inside her head like rocks in a barrel. Then she was *there*—reaching for the clouds, praying the wings he'd built for her would let her continue to soar.

Tony knew. In one smooth motion, he rose above her, entered and pushed her past the point of no return. The rhythm of his breathing in her ears matched her own as they clung to each other, floating back to earth and the security of her bed.

Several minutes later, Tony finally pulled away and lay next to her. His hand still held one hip, his head rested just above her own. She took a deep breath and smelled his maleness, mingled with the light scent of her own perfume.

She wanted to say something wonderful to him. Something about how much she loved holding him, loved feeling the weight of his body on hers. How much she loved him. She turned toward him.

His hand tightened its hold on her hip. "Don't jump up, Carolyn. Don't run away too soon. You have plenty of time before you throw yourself on that altar you call work."

She clamped her mouth shut. His words had just brought back last night's discussion.

Tony sighed, and she knew he realized what had happened. "Pulling away from me already, Carolyn?" he asked sadly.

She wanted to stroke his strong, copper-skinned back. She wanted to plant a kiss at the base of his spine.

She wanted to put her arms around him and hold him tightly against her so he couldn't retreat, wouldn't go away. She *wanted* to do all of that, but did nothing. Instead, her hand dropped beside him, touching the cool, percale coverlet. It wasn't the right substitute.

When he wasn't beside her, she felt empty.

When he hadn't consulted her about his plans, she'd felt betrayed.

"You hurt me."

He didn't turn around. "How?"

"By not asking what I thought about your working as a bartender."

"Did you think you might be hurting me, when you never asked if I minded your working night after night, while I sat in the living room and read book after book?"

"That was different. You knew I worked late when we began this . . . this . . ."

"Relationship, Carolyn? Is that such a hard word to say?"

Now she felt his frustration as well as her own. Tony was right. She was afraid of it. "Don't stray from the point, Tony. You knew I worked late every night. I didn't tell you after the fact."

"And my helping a friend at the bar is 'after the fact,' so you have every right to be angry about it?"

"I do, when you never said a word to me about it. Besides you knew what I did for a living before we started this *relationship*."

"It doesn't matter," Tony said wearily. "You're busy every night, anyway. You won't miss me, because you're always so caught up in your paperwork."

He stood and walked from the room without giving her another glance. Her heart ached. She wasn't any good at relationships. It was better not to let Tony know how important he had become to her. It would hurt less when she finally lost him.

When he returned to the bedroom with two cups of coffee, she smiled and accepted one, sipping carefully at the hot brew.

She felt his questioning gaze, his hurt, even his satisfaction at the way she'd responded to his intimacy. She couldn't—wouldn't—answer or confirm any of them, even if it broke her heart.

TONY LOOKED EXCITED when she returned home that night. "Take off tomorrow and come with me to see some property," he finally said as they cleaned up the kitchen.

"I can't, you know that," she said, wiping off a counter. "Besides, what's so special about this property? You've looked at sites for the past two months."

"This has everything I want. The real estate agent told me about it over the phone." Hands at her waist,

One More Time   163

he turned her around. "Come with me, Carolyn. I want you there when I first see it."

"What if it's not the property you want?"

He shrugged. "Then it's not, and we've both had a day off."

She was tempted. Tony drew her closer. "You need a day playing hooky," he said teasingly. "It's good for you."

After a kiss that made her head spin, Carolyn called her secretary and told her she was taking a day off.

The next morning they dressed in shorts, T-shirts and sneakers and headed out Highway 6 toward a charming little town called Chapel Hill. Tony drove and Carolyn navigated.

"Turn right here," she ordered and they left the highway for a smaller side road. Giant oaks spread their branches and sheltered the pavement from the sun. Even larger pine trees formed a second canopy. "We go a mile and a quarter," she said, peering out the windshield and loving the view. Just yards behind them was civilization, and in front lay the countryside, pure and sweet. Covering the distance quickly, they found a large white gate open, as if waiting for them. Across the top was the name Hacienda del Sol—House of the Sun.

Tony turned into the driveway, slowing down as they passed over the cattle guard. "Nice name."

"Hmm," she said, agreeing but too busy looking around to talk. She was enchanted with what she could see of the grounds. They rounded a hill, and there was an unpainted gazebo, sitting on the edge of an oval pond, surrounded by meadows of grass and wildflowers that reached as far as the eye could see behind the old, wooden-staked fence.

They reached a plateau and Carolyn gasped. A white, plantation-style, three-storied house stood on the top of the hill. Oleander bushes in brilliant pink bloom surrounded two sides and a porch wrapped around the remainder of the house. Stained glass windows above the double front doors glistened in the sunlight.

Carolyn looked at Tony, then back at the house. It wasn't until they reached the front entrance that she saw the peeling paint and buckled wood on the porch.

Tony killed the engine, they got out of the car and stood on the steps.

Tony seemed to be taking in every detail, and the more he saw the more he appeared enchanted. Carolyn tried to follow the direction of his gaze, but the more she saw, the more she became aware that there were enormous repairs to be done.

"Have you got the key?" he asked, holding out his hand.

She handed it to him, then followed Tony, stepping carefully. He walked up the steps to the front door and fitted the key into the lock. The door swung open on creaky hinges, exposing wooden floors and a foyer large enough to hold a quartet and five or six dancing couples.

They walked in silence to an enormous living area that led first to an atrium, then to the kitchen, dining room and back to the foyer. Tony approached the circular staircase with caution, but the wood appeared to be solid and there were no immediate problems. They toured the second floor, finding six bedrooms and two baths, then continued to the attic, which held another three bedrooms and a bath, as well as an enormous amount of storage space.

Tony wiped away some of the grime on one of the dormer windows overlooking the back of the property and stared out. "The house sits on thirty-two acres," he murmured, as if talking to himself.

Carolyn stood next to him and looked out, seeing a swimming pool and three more buildings. One looked like a barn, the second might perhaps be a combination of pool house and apartment. The third was a four-car garage. All were in a state of disrepair.

"I've never seen anything standing that needs as much repair as this place does." Carolyn kept her tone neutral. She knew Tony had fallen in love with the house. She hated it.

"This isn't bad," he murmured. He turned to her, his face alive with the possibilities. "Did you know this used to be a hotel back in the thirties?"

"Do you know this needs more work than you have time and money?"

"No. It's perfect."

"Tony," she said, her hands extended. "Take a look around. This place is a mess! I bet the plumbing alone will have to be completely replaced."

Tony walked back down the staircase, Carolyn on his heels. "Most plumbing needs repair after fifty years or more, darlin'."

"And the wallpaper," she added, pointing, even though he couldn't see her. "You'll have to redo every wall in the house, to say nothing of insulation."

"I'd be renovating, not restoring." Tony's tone was dry.

"What's the difference? You'll still have to plunk down a bunch of money."

"The difference in cost is about half. Restoration means to replace it just as it was. Renovating means updating it, even as you make it look its age."

"Tony, think about this," she persisted, suddenly more afraid than she'd been since she met him. "You're an hour from the Galleria area. Everything will be more expensive out here. It's too far away from the city to be profitable."

Tony walked into the kitchen and opened the cabinets, one by one. His sneakered feet stepped carefully over the rolled and torn linoleum. "It's like one of those movies—like a money pit," she declared, hands on her hips as she surveyed the gray room. "You don't need something like this, Tony. If you want a hotel, buy one. But not this."

"Why not?"

"Because . . ." She couldn't think of any other reasons. She wouldn't admit that just standing in the middle of this large kitchen gave her the chills. And she knew why. It was because she could see Tony here—without her. She couldn't possibly live here and commute. "Because it would cost too much to turn this into one. Besides, who would want to come out this far? No corporation I know."

"Carolyn, why are you so down on this project?"

She couldn't tell him. "Tony this place isn't for you."

"I'd ask you why not, but I think I already know."

"Why?" she asked, surprised.

"Because you think I should be inside the city limits. You also believe that physical labor, getting your hands dirty, isn't the kind of work I should do. You want me to buy something already fixed up and ready to roll."

Tony turned away and stared out the back bay window. "But I want something just like this. Something that I can put my stamp on, make my own."

"Why can't you build something from scratch?"

"Because I want to redo something, Carolyn, not design something. And because I want to get out of the city and the rat race that goes with it."

"Are you going to buy this place?"

Tony ran a hand through his hair. "I don't know, Carolyn. I haven't made up my mind yet."

Relief flooded her body. "Well, you don't have to decide today, do you?"

"No, not today." His tone was resigned. "Let's go."

"There are other jobs, Tony. You'll find one you like."

"I've chosen what I want. It just so happens that the woman in my life thinks she knows better than I do what I should be doing."

"Is that so wrong? Sometimes a friend can see what you're too close to see."

"And sometimes a *friend* is wearing blinders," he answered, walking out of the kitchen, heading for the front door.

She didn't take offence. After all, they were leaving. He wasn't buying this. Not now. Maybe never.

9

TRY AS SHE MIGHT to pretend otherwise, Carolyn knew their difference of opinion about his "job" threatened their future. Ever since the trip to Chapel Hill, they hadn't spoken more than a few words to each other. Neither seemed to want to be the first to admit there was anything wrong.

She lost her edge at work. After all, Tony was on her mind every waking moment of the day.

The nights were worse. Every moment she sat in her study and tried to concentrate on her paperwork, she imagined Tony standing behind a bar, surrounded by other women. No matter what she tried to think about, she wound up with the same image: Tony at a singles bar. She was childishly angry, jealous, and very, very frightened.

To her mind, Tony was hers.

As far as Tony was concerned, he was his own man.

To some female customer he was fair game.

She didn't know what to do, felt miserable about the situation, but still went on ignoring the tangled state of her emotions.

When Tony drove her to work, he laughed and joked all the way, leaving her in front of her building with a smile. But once in her office, she lost her sense of humor entirely, if the expression on her secretary's face was anything to go by. And Carolyn couldn't concentrate, try as she might. So she'd end up bundling the papers and taking them home with her, planning to work right after her lonely dinner and the news.

That didn't work, either.

Every evening Tony wasn't there she would stare into space, her mind occupied with her fear and inability to involve herself in Tony's life. No matter how much she tried to tell herself that Tony wasn't Mike, she knew what singles bars were like. Mike hadn't needed much tempting, Tony was having temptation thrown at him. How long would it be before he succumbed to a woman who wanted the same things he did? When Tony left, it might be too hard to turn off her emotions. She would never recover.

And she was sure that he would leave. His own impatience with her behavior would see to that.

So she stared out the window at the pool and wished she could work, sleep, or at least feel numb. Once in bed, she would wait for Tony, listen for his footsteps. Only after he climbed into bed could she sleep.

At the end of two weeks, Carolyn's life was a mess. She was barely keeping up with her work load—her own clients' quarterly payments to the Internal Revenue were due—and that didn't include the other clients she'd promised to take care of. They'd now been foisted onto a new junior accountant, who was probably already overworked. Carolyn's only consolation was that she had once been in that position herself; after all, it was the test by which promotions were made. She promised herself to give praise aloud for work well-done.

The lack of jealousy she felt for someone who might be climbing to her own level surprised her. It was amazing how much she was changing. But not enough.

One night, Carolyn finally couldn't stand the situation any longer. She said a prayer, got into her car and headed for the bar.

The valet parking station was closed, and the parking lot was filled to capacity. The place was obviously a huge success. She parked across the street in a business parking lot, then dodged traffic as she scooted over the main thoroughfare.

One of the latest tunes was blaring out, growing louder as she came closer. Two men, looking more like bouncers than greeters, stood at the double doors, flirting with a young girl who seemed to be all smiles and tight jeans.

Carolyn hesitated. Was she doing the right thing? Would Tony think she was spying? No matter how she played it, "just visiting" didn't really describe what she was doing here.

"Welcome to Players." The young girl smiled at her.

Carolyn smiled back. "Thanks. Is there a cover charge?"

"Only for the guys." She gave the bouncers a teasing look. "They'll follow where there's any good-looking chick," she explained with a laugh. "Enjoy yourself. There are three corner bars and a bar in the center of the dance floor. Happy hour just ended, but the buffet is still set up and free."

Carolyn nodded and began the long walk inside. She stood for a moment at the entrance to the large room and let her eyes adjust to the dimness. The walls and ceilings were black, with pink, blue, purple and green neon running around them. The posters on the walls were all of old movies and even older movie stars. The lighting was a replica of the type used on a TV or movie set. Having taken in the decor, her gaze went straight to the bars, which were well lit and crowded.

She couldn't see Tony and began to walk around the room. Passing each bar, she gave each bartender a closer look, then waited for the song to end so she could cross the dance floor and make her way to the main bar.

He wasn't there, either.

She scanned the room again. Where was he? Had he stopped working and joined some customers? Was he with friends? A woman? Panic filled her mind with all sorts of possibilities, none of them good.

At one side she saw an Exit sign; next to it was a door that bore the legend Office. Straightening her spine, Carolyn crossed the dance floor once more and headed in that direction.

She didn't have to go far. About fifty feet away from her goal, the door opened and Tony stepped out, another man at his side. They were intently engaged in conversation that only they could hear amid the loud music.

Carolyn watched every movement he made, every expression that crossed his face, and fell in love with him even more. He was wearing one of her favorite outfits: a blue-striped dress shirt open at the collar, a dark gray silk jacket with sleeves pushed up and a pair of faded jeans. It was an outfit that would never be found at the average CPA office, but it was a style of clothing that most women found dangerously attractive.

And Tony was attractive enough without the help of any designer, ponytail and all.

The two men stopped just feet from where Carolyn stood. She realized he probably hadn't seen her, for the place was packed and people were constantly walking between them.

He stared at the floor and rubbed the back of his neck as he listened to the other man. Occasionally he nodded his head or gave a quick grin. Carolyn felt her muscles slowly relax, then begin to tense again, for another reason.

She wanted to make love to him.

Swinging away from the fence, Carolyn decided it was time to let him know she was here. Perhaps he'd come home with her now.

Maybe.... She took a step toward him, but someone else beat her to his side. A beautiful woman. She was dressed all in black from her boots to the gaucho hat that crowned her thick, dark hair. Slipping her arms around the two men, she smiled and spoke to both of them, but Carolyn could tell just how much attention she was giving to Tony—a lot.

Her heart beat heavily as she saw his grin widen until she could see his dimples. He covered the other woman's hand with his own and gave it a pat, then she tugged him toward the dance floor.

Carolyn didn't want to see any more. She headed for the exit and stepped outside, breathing deeply of the fresh, moist Houston air.

People passed her as they continued to crowd into the popular night spot. She stopped for a moment, stared at the night sky and took another deep breath. Willing tears not to fall wasn't as easy as it sounded. But she tried.

Tony had been right to accuse her of confusing him with Mike. For a while she almost had. But she was intelligent enough to know better, and now the differences between the two men had been brought home.

She had played at being in love with Mike, but had never really loved him. He had been someone she'd wanted to care for, someone she'd wanted to mold into the man she'd someday have children with.

But Tony was different. She was madly, passionately, wondrously in love with him—a full-grown, adult woman in love with a full-grown, adult man. There was nothing childish about her feelings, nothing half-baked or motherly in her approach. And she wanted him to love her just as much as she loved him.

What frustrated her was the realization that she wasn't in control of this situation, at least not the way she'd been with all the other people in her life. For the first time she knew that no matter what she wanted, the end result was out of her hands. She had no control over how Tony felt, saw, acted—or over whom he loved.

Moving unsteadily, almost like a drunkard, she headed for her car and began the short drive home. She didn't have the slightest idea what she'd do once she got there.

Should she casually ask him about the woman he'd smiled at this evening? Should she not mention her foray into his world and go on pretending that everything was fine? That was what she'd done when she'd found out that Mike had been fooling around. She'd pretended that what she didn't know wouldn't hurt her.

And that behavior had put an end to her relationship with her closest friend, her sister.

Was turning her back on this problem going to resolve it?

She didn't know.

Two hours later, she still hadn't decided how to act. The sound of a car engine told her she'd run out of time. Tony was home.

Holding a glass of wine she waited tensely for him to enter the house. When he finally opened the door and came inside, Carolyn wanted to cry with relief.

For almost two hours she'd imagined him in the arms of another woman, deciding not to return to her, after all. Her nerves had been put through the wringer.

Tony must have seen her distress in spite of the dim hall lighting; he strode straight to her, taking her into his arms and holding her in silence.

A sob caught in her throat and she clung to his broad shoulders with one hand. The other tried to balance the wineglass without spilling its contents over him.

He noticed her dilemma and chuckled, then took the glass from her and set it aside. "We don't have to make a hug this difficult, darlin'," he teased, but his gaze searched her face. "What's the matter? What happened?"

Carolyn tilted her head and tried to paste a smile onto her lips. "Can't a gal wait for the guy in her life to come home?"

His hand rested on her chin, a thumb brushed at the trembling lips. "Not when she usually has work in the morning and needs her sleep."

"I'll survive," she promised. "Want a drink?"

"No, thanks." Tony stepped back and ran a hand through his hair. "It's been a rough night, but a drink isn't what I need."

"What is?" she asked, reaching for her glass.

"You."

Her hand froze in the air. Her heart skipped a beat, then dashed on faster than before. "Then what are we waiting for?"

Tony stared at her, his narrowed gaze delving deeply inside her, touching off sparks that threatened to ignite and burn her. She couldn't even hear her own breathing, her heart was pumping so hard.

"Finished with your drink?" he asked, his voice rasping in the quiet.

She reached out her hand and enveloped his. "Yes." Her own voice was equally quiet.

Without another word they turned and walked down the hallway to the bedroom. Neither turned on the light as they undressed and flipped back the comforter.

Climbing into bed, Tony propped the pillows against the headboard and lay back, taking her into the comfort of his embrace so that she rested against the broad nakedness of his chest. She sighed and some of the tension flowed away.

The pool lights played on the ceiling, picking out the fluorescent baby stars that shone here and there. Tony gently rubbed her back and arms. His chin rested on the top of her head. From time to time she felt him kiss her hair.

She'd never before felt so loved. No unfulfilled sexual fantasies, no tension needing to be released. No demons craving to be exorcised. Just pure, heavenly enjoyment filling mind and body.

Tony couldn't have spent the past two hours in some other woman's arms, only to come home and make her feel this way. It wasn't possible. She knew it; deep in the very core of her, she knew it.

"Tell me about it, Carolyn." Tony's voice broke into her reverie. He continued to caress her.

Forming the words that reflected up her worst nightmare was the hardest thing she'd ever done. "Is there any other woman in your life, Tony?"

His chuckle was dark and rueful. "I can barely keep up with *you*, and you entertain an idea that there might be another woman, Carolyn? Thanks for the compliment, but I don't think I could handle any more at this time." He hesitated, then added in a teasing voice that flowed over her dismal thoughts like honey. "Now, when I was twenty and full of . . ."

Carolyn gave him a tight hug and heard the breath whoosh out of his lungs.

He chuckled again. "Satisfied?"

"Yes," she murmured into the crinkly hair on his chest. She felt like a fool—a very happy fool. He was right. There was no other woman and, despite her doubts, she should have known that.

Tony slipped one leg familiarly between her own. "Why would you think such a thing?"

It had taken all her stamina to confront him. Now she wanted to go into hiding again. She was through. "I don't want to talk about it."

"Too late." His tone was firm.

Carolyn sighed, knowing she might as well say it now and get it over with. She rolled over and rested the back of her head against his chest, staring at her favorite star on the ceiling and silently praying that he would understand. His hand cupped her breast, one thumb absently rubbing against the tender skin as he waited for her to begin. His other hand stroked her arm, as if reassuring her that all would be well.

"I went to the club tonight and saw you with another woman."

"Why did you come to the club?"

"Because I missed you."

"I've invited you often enough, and you never 'missed me' enough to visit the bar before."

"Well, I did tonight."

"I'm flattered. I think."

"You're outrageous."

He chuckled. "Probably, So tell me, why did you visit the bar? Truth."

Knowing that Tony would pursue this line of questioning until he was satisfied, she decided to humor him, but had to force the words out. "And I saw you come out of an office, talking to some man."

The humor left his voice. "And?"

"And then a woman walked up and put her arm around you. After a minute or two, you walked her onto the dance floor."

His hand stopped stroking her and she missed the caress. His heart began to thump, hard, and hers sank to her toes. She stared at the star, making one more quick wish that this would soon be over and forgotten. Very soon. Immediately.

"I didn't realize that you might possibly be jealous. Or that I might object," he finally answered. "So, after seeing this slightly sordid display of affection, you decided there was another woman in my life and I was keeping her under wraps while I was living with you?" His voice rose as if in astonishment.

"No, but I was curious enough to ask about her." She knew she sounded defensive, but her need to know weighed more heavily than making a fool of herself.

"And being curious enough to have to ask me irritates you?"

"No. Yes."

Her body was rigid by now. Carolyn was so tense, she wondered if her muscles had turned to steel. She tried to tell herself to relax, but her body didn't respond. It probably wouldn't until he answered.

"What do you think was going on, Carolyn?" His tone was deceptively calm. Every instinct told her that he was even more upset than she.

But it was too late to backtrack. "You've asked me enough questions. You tell me."

"The man I walked out of the office with was an old business associate, a realtor. He thought he'd found a location for me. I looked at it yesterday. Tonight we were discussing the price I want to offer. That woman is his wife. I had promised her a special, nonalcoholic drink I'd invented in my youth and she was calling me on the promise. I didn't take her to the dance floor, Carolyn. I escorted her to the bar area."

She couldn't think of a single thing to say. What she wanted to do most of all was kick herself for doubting. But she could give herself one small accolade. "At least I asked, Tony. I didn't jump to conclusions."

"Oh, yes, you did."

Tony adjusted the pillows behind his back and Carolyn sat up, waiting for him to complete the task. When he'd finished, he leaned back again without taking her into his arms. It was a silent gesture of rejection and hurt so badly that tears stung her eyes.

"You're angry."

"I'm hurt," he corrected. "Every time I turn around, I'm being punished for someone else's sins, no matter what I do."

"That's not true. I never punished you!" She twisted around to confront him face-to-face. She might have done a lot of things wrong in this relationship, but not that.

He raised a questioning eyebrow. "When you forced yourself to work late on paperwork, weren't you teaching me not to expect your company, except when you wanted to give it? When you 'forgot' to call home when you went out for a drink with friends? That eliminated two needs, Carolyn. You showed me that you didn't have to check in with anyone, and that you didn't need me for your social life. Meanwhile, I was waiting at home for you. The best of all possible worlds." His self-derisive tone wounded her far more deeply than his physical retreat.

She'd been very stupid. Thinking that Tony wasn't reading her right, or at all, she'd punished one man for another man's sins. She'd known it all along, but had tried to ignore it.

"Tony, I . . ." The apology stuck in her throat. Tears pressed against her eyelids, then fell in a stream to wet her cheeks.

His resigned sigh was audible. He tried to erase a tear with his thumb, but another immediately took its place. "Don't cry," he pleaded.

She leaned forward and brushed a damp kiss upon his parted lips. "I'm sorry, Tony. I'm so sorry."

"So am I, darlin'. So am I," he whispered, one hand circling her neck and cupping an ear. His mouth brushed hers, then brushed it again. Before they knew it was happening, they were kissing desperately.

Finally Tony pulled away, resting his forehead against hers. "Come with me, Carolyn. Come with me to the country and leave this world behind."

Her throat almost closed. "Tony, I can't," she whispered in despair.

"Sure you can. You can run your accounting business from the hotel. People in the country have business needs, too." He kissed the tip of her nose. "Meanwhile, we'll be leading a slower, more fruitful life, enjoying the smell of clover, sunsets and quiet times. Maybe even have a child."

That last thought tore into her and she rebelled. Damn him! He was baiting a trap, and she resented having to choose. "Tony..."

"You'll love it, Carolyn. We'd be so happy there," he assured her, enthusiasm coloring his words.

She cleared her throat. "I can't," she said again, loud and clear.

This time he heard her. "Why?"

She held his face in her hands, trying to reach him with all the sincerity she possessed. "I've worked ten years for a partnership, Tony. I'm within a year or two of getting it. Besides, if it's a family you want, we could think about starting one here. Not all families live in the country, you know."

"You don't really want that, do you?"

"Yes," she declared firmly, though her stomach was tied in a huge knot. "I want it more than anything. I've worked hard for it. I can't just drop out of life now."

"Why not?" he retorted. "Everything you do says that you're on the edge of burnout. You don't get any enjoyment out of your job anymore. I'd venture a guess that you haven't enjoyed working for a long time. It's just a habit, Carolyn. Not a love. Most of the time you're on a treadmill, doing the same, monotonous thing over and over."

Her defenses went up. "You're wrong," she said emphatically. "I love my work. But whether I do or not, I'm not dumping everything I've worked for."

Tony sat very still, his gaze fixed on her. "Is that what you think I'm doing?"

Unable to say the words aloud, she nodded her head.

"You're wrong, Carolyn. Dead wrong."

"Tony, please try to understand."

He shook his head, sighed, and pulled her toward him. "I was hoping . . . but I should have known better. All the signs were there and I chose to ignore them." He spoke slowly, voice low, his tone resigned.

"What signs?"

"The ones that said you weren't ready for more. That marriage was out of the question." He drew her closer, and she curled against his body until they were completely entwined. "That place I took you to in Chapel Hill is exactly what I was looking for, Carolyn."

"I thought we decided that place was a mess!"

"No, darlin'. *You* decided that. I want it, and I'm signing the papers on it."

"You'll do that, even though you know I won't follow?"

Tony nodded. "You knew what I was doing from the beginning, Carolyn. I talked about my plans all the time. Unlike you, I never made a secret of them. You knew I wanted out."

Her heart thudded in her breast, heavy and slow. Tears pressed against her lids. She could see him out there, enjoying life. Who cared if he was hiding? He was doing it his way. There was an awful lot to be said for that. But he'd be doing it alone. God! That thought hurt!

"I'm building eight miniature versions of the original house and then renting them out to company executives for board meetings, special events and small seminars."

She waited until she could trust herself to speak. "Sounds delightful." Even to her, the words sounded hollow.

"It's perfect," he said softly. "I'll be able to handle my investments by phone, cook to my heart's delight, and enjoy the rest of my life, living the way I want to live."

There was nothing else she could say. He'd always said that was what he wanted. He'd always been upfront. If she hadn't discussed her own needs, well, that was her fault. She'd just assumed that he knew her feelings. Apparently she'd been wrong.

Finally she asked the question she dreaded most. "When are you moving?"

"If the paperwork moves quickly, I'll be in the house by next week."

Silence hung heavy in the room. Even though she'd turned down his offer, Carolyn had expected him to propose marriage. He'd asked her everything but that. In fact, she'd expected him to fight harder than he had. She'd expected anything—except the silence that had wedged itself between them like a thick wall.

"I'll miss you," she ventured. "So much."

"I love you." Tony's voice was deep and sure and filled with sadness. "So much."

She wanted to tell him she loved him, too, but couldn't. She moved her lips, but the words wouldn't form themselves into sounds. They couldn't.

"Don't worry." Tony leaned forward and kissed the top of her head. "No answer is needed, Carolyn. Silence is as much of a declaration as words."

He gave her a hug and slipped out of her arms.

Carolyn sat up, letting the sheet drop to her waist. "Where are you going?"

"For a swim," he said. He strode naked across the room and opened the sliding glass doors. "Go to sleep. I'll be back soon."

Then he was out the door and it swished shut behind him. Two seconds later he dived into the pool and began swimming with long, even strokes that took him from one end to the other and back again.

Carolyn's gaze was glued to every gliding movement. Even from her vantage point she could see the tension in his form.

What would she do without Tony in her life? She wanted him to understand that her behavior wasn't really a guide to the way she felt, deep inside. She needed him to take her into his life, his heart, mistakes and all.

Most of all, she craved for him to ask her to marry him, knowing that if he asked, she wouldn't change her answer. She still couldn't.

All the way through this alliance, she'd made goof after goof. But even if she had a chance to do things over again, she wasn't sure what she would do to make the story end differently. Her brother was right; she didn't know what she wanted early enough in a relationship to make a difference.

If the air-conditioning hadn't kicked on, sending the sound rumbling through the house, Carolyn would have sworn she'd heard her heart break.

10

IF CAROLYN HAD THOUGHT her personal life couldn't get any worse, she was wrong. Every day for the next week she walked into an empty house. Busy closing the deal, Tony returned home much later than usual, full of plans. He wanted to tell her about the renovations, the problems and the highlights of the work he was having done, but the more excited he grew, the more she retreated into her own world. Each job completed on the house in Chapel Hill meant that Tony was a day closer to leaving.

Knowing she was acting childishly, she refused to talk about his house or his plans for leaving. If she didn't acknowledge the situation, then he wouldn't go. After several aborted attempts, Tony stopped pressing her to discuss the matter. Instead, they kept quiet during the time they were together, their only contact making love, frantically, silently, in the dark of night.

Late one Friday afternoon her boss, Jeff Harden, called her into the conference room, where she found the other three partners in the firm. Her heart sank. Were they going to let her go? Then anger supplanted the immediate fear and she tilted her chin daringly, taking her time to look each of them in the eye. They stared back.

Until Tony had entered her life, she'd done more work than any other certified public accountant in the company. She'd given her entire personal life to her work. She was still an excellent employee. If the gentlemen wanted to chastise her for not working as hard now, it would take all three of them and more to negate her past record.

Mr. Freeman, the founder of the company, spoke up. "Ms. Perkins, you know in what high esteem your ability is held in our little office. Jeff Harden has relayed our kudos to you on numerous occasions, I'm sure."

Surprised, Carolyn looked at Jeff, but his gaze was glued to the pages in front of him, as if he were memorizing the figures printed there.

"Despite the quarterly report deadlines, we still had to arrange this meeting to congratulate you on your constantly superior and occasionally brilliant work for us."

She tried not to show her shock. Where was all this conversation and praise leading? If she was being fired, it was the most unusual firing she'd ever heard of.

"And so we are offering you a partnership in the company, beginning Monday of next week. Along with it will come all the advantages of owning a part of such a prestigious and traditional company such as ours, including a share of the profits." Mr. Freeman leaned back, looking self-satisfied. "So, Ms. Perkins. What do you have to say?"

Her mind stopped working for a brief moment, then kicked in again, scrambling in every direction like a hyperactive child. She tried to calm her thoughts but nothing worked. Growing frantic, she stared at the CEO, feeling like an idiot.

If this offer had been made just one month ago, everyone would have known her reply instantly. But not now.

The silence turned from comfortable to tense as the four men waited for Carolyn to say something. She moved her lips, but no sound came out.

"Ms. Perkins? Are you all right?" one of the partners asked.

Clearing her throat, she forced herself to smile. "I'm fine, just overwhelmed, that's all."

Apparently satisfied with her answer, they visibly relaxed. "Well, what do you say?"

She'd worked so hard for this honor, this money—both of the ingredients necessary to her measure of success. Now she couldn't seem to form her thoughts into a coherent pattern. Finally realizing what they were waiting for, she gave them the answer she'd rehearsed in her dreams. "I'm honored and delighted to accept. Thank you."

Why didn't this moment have more impact? Why wouldn't her brain stop screaming *No*? She was insane to even entertain a thought of turning down what she had worked so hard for all her adult life!

After a few more teasing remarks and a repetition of some of the privileges that came with becoming a part-ner, Carolyn shook hands with everyone, then left the room in a daze.

Her secretary was smiling broadly, but Carolyn saw the smile fade as she walked past the desk and into her office, very carefully closing her door with the admo-nition, "Please hold all calls for a while."

Instead of sitting in her own chair, Carolyn chose one of the wing chairs on the other side of the rosewood desk. It was the chair most of her clients sat in when they visited the office. Sitting there now, she saw her work area from their point of view.

She stared at the work center. It consisted of two computers, one perched above the other. File folders of work pending were neatly stacked on the other side, by the telephone console. Everything was neat and or-derly. Everything was workable. Everything was so damn efficient.

"This is the office of Carolyn Perkins, our partner," she imagined Jeff saying to a customer. "Her office is right next to our library because she uses it so often."

It sounded superperfectionist, and was exactly that. She deserved this promotion. She'd worked harder than any two men in this firm. So where was the joy? Where was the satisfaction?

A sharp tap at the door made her jump. Before she could speak to send anyone away, Jeff stuck his head around the door, then stepped in. "Why aren't you ordering champagne and oysters? Why aren't you telling everyone in the office about your good news? Mr. Freeman purposely kept it a secret from everyone except your secretary so you could make your own announcement."

"How kind of him."

Jeff looked incredulous. "Are you being sarcastic?"

Carolyn sighed. "No, of course not. I'm just still in a state of shock, Jeff." She leaned over and patted the matching wing chair. "Sit down and talk to me. Tell me why they chose this particular time to make me a partner."

Jeff looked a little wary as he slid into the seat. He laughed nervously. "Most people would be thrilled to be a partner. They'd never worry about what time it was."

"Except me. Come on, Jeff. Give me a clue."

He held up his hands. "Okay, okay, I give." He wriggled in the chair for a second, then looked at her over his hands, fingertips pressed together. "I knew you were getting impatient, waiting for us to offer you a partnership, so I put the bug into Mr. Freeman's ear."

As far as she knew, Jeff had never shown consideration or concern before, unless there was something for him in a given proposal. But he was always willing to take the credit for something good. "Why?" she persisted.

"Because I didn't want the company to lose you, and I knew you were becoming dissatisfied with the wait."

Carolyn understood. "Because I wasn't doing as much work as I used to?"

Jeff shifted uncomfortably. "Something like that."

"And did you think that I might have been contemplating another offer?"

He shifted again. "Were you?"

She smiled. "No."

Standing, he gave her a smile of relief. "Well, then we don't have to worry about that, do we? We all got what we wanted. You have your partnership and understand how much we value you. And we have a valuable, hardworking partner, who will help bring in more business."

Watching him turn away brought a grin of satisfaction to her face. "What a great combination."

"It is, isn't it?" he said as he strolled to the door and opened it. "Don't forget to tell the office."

"I'll do it in my own time, Jeff."

He hesitated in the doorway, only his head still visible. "When?"

"Next week," she hedged. "With champagne . . . the works."

His delight was evident. "I'll tell the other partners. By the way, congratulations."

"Thanks."

Then he was gone.

Carolyn sat down again and contemplated Jeff's confession. What an odd turn of events! She'd actually gotten the promotion she'd worked so hard for by not working so hard!

Work had given her her sense of purpose. She'd loved being needed, and had been satisfied to help her clients. Performing any important service had given her that feeling, but now she just wasn't sure it was enough for her anymore.

Not caring that it wasn't even close to five o'clock, she grabbed her purse, told her secretary she'd be gone, and left the office.

She needed to see Tony. She wanted him to listen while she talked out her feelings. Then he would curl his arms around her, holding her securely against the demons of the night. But most of all she wanted to make love with him, to celebrate the mystery of life with him.

She wanted—needed—to tell him that she loved him.

When she arrived home, his car was gone. But that was all right, she told herself. He'd be home later. She went straight to the bedroom and stripped off her suit jacket. Carolyn opened the closet door, then stood stock-still and stared at the empty space.

Half the closet was empty. All Tony's clothes were gone. Light dawned and she whirled around, her gaze darting all over the room until it landed on a white envelope that lay on the chest at the foot of her bed.

She walked to it with slow steps. Her name was written across the front in Tony's bold print.

Tears filmed her eyes.

He was gone.

No matter what the letter inside the envelope said, Tony had moved out.

Her thoughts skipped back to the moment, earlier that morning, when she had awakened to her usual cup of hot coffee sitting on the nightstand, and to Tony, sitting on the side of the bed. She'd been able to tell by the cloudy look in his blue eyes that he was disturbed about something, and had even had an idea what it was. But she hadn't wanted to hear it, so she'd leaned forward and nuzzled his neck instead.

Responding instantly, his arms had enclosed her in a soft, gentle hug, holding her as if she were more precious than gold. It had been so reassuring that she'd felt he might have changed his mind about moving.

The half-empty closet was proof of how wrong she had been.

It also hinted at how lonely her future would be.

Carolyn sat on the edge of the bed, still staring at the crisp white envelope. When her eyes burned from looking at it, she leaned back and stared at the ceiling instead. Over and over she told herself that he would return, but knew better. Her heart knew better. Finally tears fell.

Around four o'clock in the morning Carolyn finally drifted into a nightmare-filled sleep. This time the nightmares had nothing to do with her sister or past marriage, but everything to do with Tony.

The envelope lay untouched.

THAT WEEKEND was the loneliest Carolyn ever remembered spending. Unwilling to cave in to self-pity, she visited her brother's home Saturday afternoon. Her nieces were darling, and Tammy's sturdy smile and easy ways were comforting. Ed was on the golf course.

After sharing the day with them, Carolyn dressed in a new outfit and forced herself to meet a few associates for drinks and dinner, then attended a play she'd been wanting to see. She was home by midnight, in bed by twelve-fifteen.

The letter was still unopened.

Sunday morning, she watched her favorite television programs, then put on her best jogging suit and power-walked around Memorial Park's trails. When she returned, she repotted several plants, worked in the backyard, then changed and went to dinner at her favorite restaurant.

That night she swam until her arm muscles quivered. Exhausted, she fell into bed.

Staring at the ceiling, she forced herself to think of the things about Tony that irritated her, like his leaving his socks in a pile by the side of the bed or never putting the soup spoons where they belonged. His ponytail was another of those mixed blessings. She loved his long hair and the glances it got, but hated the glances it raked from other females, who showed by their expressions that they believed he was dangerously outrageous. And sexy.

Other memories came faster, easy to recollect. Impromptu bedroom picnics, Tony's open enjoyment of showering with her, delicious meals, during which one word—any silly word he chose for the evening—was not allowed to be spoken. His playful, wonderful, intense lovemaking.

Around two in the morning, she knew what she missed most about Tony.

His loving presence.

MONDAY MORNING dawned dreary, rainy. Carolyn selected her best suit, highest heels, pulled back her hair into a French twist that wouldn't allow a single strand even to think of loosening.

After a few cups of coffee she repacked her attaché case, reached for her courage and picked up Tony's letter. She'd spent the entire weekend mourning the loss of the man she loved. There was nothing else she could do. Now it was time to get on with life.

She unfolded the letter and stared at it, holding her breath to keep the pain at bay.

His bold print looked neat and orderly on the stark white paper. But it was his message that wrapped itself too tightly around her heart. She quickly scanned it once, then read it slowly.

Darlin',
The house is ready to move in, and the architects' plans for other additions are complete. It will keep me busy. I wish I was the man for you like you are the only woman for me. But we both know differently, don't we?

If you ever decide to leave the rat race, know that I'm waiting. But I can't live with a foot in both worlds.

If you ever want to be with me, you know where I am.

If not, then remember that I love you as much as any man can love a woman.

P.S. I have your diamond earring again. It's now mine. In a day or so, the jewelers will deliver replacements.

Written at the bottom were his address and phone number.

Tears streamed down her face before she even finished the letter. Carolyn closed her eyes. She could hear him saying the words, see his sad, blue-eyed expression as he looked at her.

She'd prevented him from getting involved in her life, but not because she was ashamed of him. She hadn't wanted to share him. Barely able to cope with the rigorous business schedule she'd set for herself, she'd taken respite by hiding both of them from prying, public eyes.

Damn the man for leaving her with this empty feeling and then telling her that he loved her completely! What nerve! Who the hell did he think he was, taking advantage of her that way? He'd infiltrated her personal life, making her feel happy for the first time she could remember! He'd used companionship, touching and laughter as crutches to pursue their relationship!

Carolyn took a deep breath. Now life had returned to the same routine it had had "Before Tony," and she ought to be able to slip right into the rhythm of it.

She'd do it, too, if it killed her!

Carefully holding on to her anger, Carolyn strode into her office and began to plan an office party. Her secretary helped with the arrangements. At the end of next week they would be the hostesses at her promotion party.

It wasn't until a courier delivered a beautiful set of two-carat diamond earrings that she began to understand what Tony had meant.

She had to laugh. Tony must have taken one more step toward being outrageous. She'd bet he'd had his ear pierced!

Her laughter stopped abruptly as she clutched the new earrings to her breast. They highlighted just how much she missed him. Everything was on hold as long as Tony was out of her life.

Just a few months ago she'd been sure that they were not meant to be together, that it was only a matter of time before they would break up.

Now she knew just how silly she'd been. She'd shown no foresight at all. Tony had worked his way into her life, her heart, without letting her suspect a thing. In six short months he'd become the close friend that Cora had been—and more of a lover than Mike had ever dreamed of becoming. He'd also filled the shoes of her father by sharing his wisdom with her, and then had displayed the gentle caring her mother had never given.

And in those same six months she'd never shared anything with him other than her home and body. Giving didn't seem to be her strong point.

Moving quickly, decisively, she switched the earrings he'd sent her with the one that remained of the original pair. Grabbing her purse, Carolyn headed out the door. She needed to see Tony. Now.

The drive to Chapel Hill seemed to take forever. Traffic dawdled on the road, acting as if it were a Sunday.

When she finally turned into the fenced property, she was stunned. Neatly trimmed grass ran over the hill and down to the pond. The fence and gazebo were a fresh, clean white against the green, fit to be shown on a picture postcard.

The house gave her the biggest surprise of all. As she drove slowly over the hill, the first thing she saw was the penny-new, copper roof gleaming in the sun. Then the rest came into view. The house was now clad in bright white and lemon yellow. All the rotten wood, birds' nests, dirt and rubbish were gone. The windows gleamed in the sunlight, especially the two stained glass works of art above the door.

Off to one side of the driveway stood several pickup trucks filled with odd pieces of lumber, insulation and other items Carolyn wasn't familiar with. Somewhere in the distance the sound of a buzz saw ripped through the air.

She walked up the steps to the door and knocked. When no one answered, she turned the old-fashioned doorbell. Still no answer.

She walked around to the side porch, scanning the well-tended grounds as she went. When she reached the back, the pool caught her eye. All the thick, dirty water had been drained away and someone was down on the bottom, recementing the sides.

Tony stood less than two feet from her.

He must have heard her at the same time as she saw him. When he swung around, his expression, stern at first, turned into the biggest, sexiest smile she'd ever seen. It warmed her all the way to her toes.

"Carolyn!"

His arms encircled her waist and he drew her close. His mouth came down upon hers in a kiss that was as demanding as it was sensuous. Every fiber in her being answered.

He pulled away, too soon. "I knew you'd change your mind."

Before she could answer, he wrapped an arm around her waist again and led her inside by the back door. "Come on. I want you to see what's been completed so far."

If she'd been startled by the outside of the house, the inside was positively astounding! Deep forest green and stark white tile checkered the vast expanse of the kitchen floor. Cabinets, once dingy, were now laminated a bright white and had been given clear glass insets that highlighted their contents. Deep peach-toned dishes, glasses and canisters all added to the atmosphere, making the room modern, cozy and warm.

"I don't believe it!" Carolyn exclaimed; she turned and stared at the room again and again.

Tony's laughter echoed around the room. "It's different from the last time you saw it, isn't it?"

"Different!" she exclaimed. "This looks like a page out of *Architectural Digest*. Before it looked like something out of Junk For Sale ads!"

He stood behind her. "Does that mean you like it?"

"Of course."

His lips touched her neck. "I'm glad." He took her hand and led her to the hallway, into the foyer and toward the stairs. "Come see the bedroom. We just finished the walls and floor."

The foyer's wainscoting caught her eye as they walked through and headed up the stairs. The wainscoting had been stripped, the wallpaper steamed off. The ceiling had been newly shackled and the chandelier, probably brand-new, hung in place.

The circular staircase, she noted fleetingly, had also been sanded and varnished.

The change in the bedroom was remarkable. Five windows marched across the back and side of the room, each one holding fourteen panes, beautifully held together by leaden beads. The walls were of wainscoting, the wood painted a pale tan, the wall above heavily shackled in a shade darker than that of the wainscoting. Beautifully designed molding marched around the perimeter of the ceiling. The wooden plank flooring had been redone, too, then pickled, with streaks of white coating.

"It's beautiful, Tony. Absolutely beautiful."

He sat down on the only piece of furniture in the room, a straight-backed chair that stood in one corner. "So are you," he said quietly. "Come here."

Carolyn walked toward him, stopping when she stood between his knees. Suddenly she felt shy and awkward. Then she saw what had brought her here in the first place.

Putting her hand into her pocket, she pulled out her gift. "Here's the other, in case you need a spare."

"So you guessed what I did with it," he chuckled; and the sound vibrated down her back to sensitize her responses. "Now I have a spare. Thanks."

"It wasn't hard to guess when you took only one," she declared. His voice sounded wonderful. "Besides, doesn't it go with a ponytail?"

"It also goes with piracy, but I haven't begun to scour the high seas for booty," he answered.

"So, have you scoured for anything else lately?"

His hands rested on her hips, warming her skin right through the fabric. "Apparently not enough of anything that matters, or I wouldn't be the only person for miles around."

"What do you mean?" she asked.

"If I were great at this, I'd have enough female captives to be able to entertain a different one every night. Instead, the only female company I have is a delivery woman, who has a better set of muscles than I have."

Once again Tony made her laugh. It had been two weeks since she'd seen or heard from him, and she'd forgotten what a great human being he was. Her mind taunted her with so many memories, but not one held a candle to reality.

"Poor baby," she crooned, pretending she didn't have a lump in her throat from the tears that threatened. "Then you need to take your mind off women by paying more attention to turning your business into a profit maker." She ran a hand over the side of his head, finally resting it on his shoulder. She needed to feel him, touch him. Love him.

"I need your expertise with numbers to help me."

It was good to know that he respected her skills, but she wanted him to love and want her so much that he would return to her home. Deep in her heart she knew he wouldn't come back. But she wanted to try. "You can hire anyone to do the books."

"Sure," he drawled, "but can they make babies, too?"

There was silence. Her heart stopped pounding for a moment, only to restart with an erratic beat. "Babies?" she repeated, knowing she sounded like a parrot.

"You know, those cute little animals that grow up to be sassy big animals?"

She knew what happened to her pounding heart then. It jumped straight into her throat. She tried to pass off his comment as a joke. "What are you doing, Tony? Soliciting wombs?"

"No," he said patiently. "I already tried to talk a certain woman I'm in love with into leaving humdrum work to live a fuller life at a slower pace."

"Sounds like you want a surrogate mother."

"I just want you, Carolyn."

"You're so definite about what you want," she finally managed.

"I know what makes me happy. Don't you?"

Tears filled her eyes. How did he know so much, while she was only beginning to learn? "What makes you happy?"

He didn't hesitate; his voice was strong and sure. "Having you at my side, playing, laughing, crying and living. Married or unmarried. Flaws and all."

She still couldn't think. Earlier she'd wanted him to propose, but now that he had and happiness was within reach, she didn't know if she had the nerve to reach out and grab it. "Whose flaws?"

"Both of ours." It was said with firm belief and she knew he was right. He'd accepted her idiosyncrasies, but she'd never dealt with his.

Carolyn said the only thing that came to mind. "I was given a partnership in the firm last week."

Tony's long sigh summed up everything she felt. "I see. Well, I guess that answers my question."

"I can't leave my work, Tony, but you could move back with me," she ventured, at last finding the nerve to say what she'd been thinking ever since he'd left.

"I'm staying here, Carolyn. I'm not getting into the rat race again."

"Tony, I . . ." She stopped, unsure what to say.

"Don't worry, darlin'. I'll survive." His voice was hollow, echoing the sound of her heart. When his hands left her hips, she felt bereft.

"I told you I needed work, Tony. People count on me."

"According to you, work is hard, Carolyn. There's no law that says that work can't be play, too. Raising a family, running a business from your home are work, too."

"Don't!" she cried, almost choking. Pictures flashed into her head—pictures of her daydreams that had never come to fruition because she'd been too busy. Or because she hadn't known exactly what would make her happy.

"I was wrong about you. I always thought you were afraid to make a commitment. But it wasn't the commitment you couldn't make, it was the commitment *to me.* I bet you had no problem saying yes to your partnership." Tony's words sounded flat, as if they came from far away. "I wish you luck, Carolyn. You got what you really wanted."

He stood and walked to the window, staring out at the pastoral scene. She watched the sunlight play on his hair, black and white shadows throwing his features into relief. Until this moment she'd never realized just how much she loved him. More than she could put into words. More than she could show.

How in the world could she tell him about her feelings at that moment? She tried, forming thoughts into words before uttering them.

Just as she was about to open her mouth, Tony turned his back on her completely. "Goodbye, Carolyn. Have a good life."

It was a dismissal. Tony had just excluded her from his life.

Instead of tears, anger flared, deep inside. "*Damn you*, Tony!"

She stormed out of the room and down the stairs. She jumped into the car and started the engine, her foot heavy on the gas. Tires flung out gravel as she spun around and headed for Houston. Her home. Her way of life.

She was halfway home when she realized that driving the car like a maniac might feel good, but it didn't erase the overwhelming sense of emptiness that Tony's absence had created.

Nothing would.

She slowed down and took her time returning to her empty house.

THE FRIDAY MORNING of her office party marked the passage of two long days since she'd spoken to Tony. Two days filled with hectically paced work and tears at every private moment. She'd relived their conversation over and over again, using it to whip herself into action. Not a moment had gone by when she wasn't evaluating everything she'd thought she knew against what she knew she felt. Never having known exactly what she'd need in her personal life, Carolyn felt like a kid setting up her own punishment. Now she had to look hard at her crime of not paying early attention to that area of her life, then decide what to do about it.

Everything pointed back to her early years: she had craved a home, a family, a closeness with a partner like that she'd had with her siblings. And more. Much more.

Now she wanted love—Tony's love.

But was she willing to give up everything for it?

After a busy morning at business, caterers came and set up a lunch buffet in the conference room that impressed even the partners. Champagne flowed, salmon and caviar, pâté and sauces were set out with a carefully calculated abandon. A small chamber group sat in the reception area and played background music.

Employees made a half-day party out of the affair, laughing and enjoying the food, the music and the time off.

Carolyn stepped into her office, leaving the door open; she listened to the voices and music and wondered what in heaven's name she was doing. This morning she'd even stunned herself by pulling out of the driveway, then cutting the engine and staring at her home. Suddenly she didn't want it anymore. Tired of keeping it up by herself, she wanted something simpler. Or someone to share it with.

Jeff Harden strolled in, a smug grin on his face and a half-filled champagne glass in his hand. "I told those guys you knew how to throw a party, Carolyn. And I was right. My instincts are always dead center."

"Really?" Arms crossed, she turned her back on the window and faced him. "Then maybe you could tell me what instincts told you not to give me the kind words the partners thought they'd passed along?"

Jeff laughed nervously. "Now, you know as well as I do that you work better without all that folderol."

"I see. How kind of you to notice," she said dryly. Finally it had dawned on her that Jeff had always been able to manipulate her. Funny that today was the first time she'd really noticed it.

Time and Tony had changed her. She wasn't as easily led now—either that, or she was looking for a bigger carrot to work for. She shivered. The idea of someone putting a carrot in front of her and watching her run toward it was horrendous.

"Now, Carolyn, don't pretend that I hurt your feelings. You've always enjoyed your work. At least you used to," Jeff amended. "I'm hoping that you'll get back into the groove, now that you've got your partnership and the party's over."

She tilted her head and stared at him, as if seeing him for the first time. "I worked fifty-five hours this week. What kind of groove do you want me to get back into?"

He shrugged, looking somewhere over her shoulder rather than at her. "You know. Back to traveling again and helping out a little more with the overload." He sat down in one of the wing chairs and drank the rest of his champagne. "I'm leaving for Europe next month, and I want to make sure that everything's under control."

"How nice." She made her smile syrupy sweet. "How long will you be gone?"

"A month." Carolyn raised her brows, and he quickly continued. "Well, you know, when you spend that much money to get there, you might as well stay a while."

"How true," she commiserated.

He relaxed again.

"Don't you have exclusivity with the DuPree account?" she asked. It was the biggest account in their office and brought in a pretty penny, for both the office and Jeff's pocket. "And isn't it due next month?"

Jeff smiled. "That's right. But they'll deal with you, now that you're a partner. I've got a meeting scheduled for Tuesday. I'll take you with me and get everything settled then."

"Why me? Why not one of the other partners?" She knew what he was going to say, even before he said it. She felt as if she were in a time warp, knowing what was going to happen before it did. Why had she never seen things so clearly before?

"They have their own accounts to maintain. Besides, you'll just be handling the paperwork for a month or so, then I'll be back to take over."

He didn't have to state the obvious: if the other partners did any work, they'd expect a piece of the profits. But Jeff plainly thought that Carolyn would not only do the work, but continue to give him the credit.

She'd worked for the company for over ten years and never taken off more than three days at a time. Never. She knew it wasn't Jeff's fault, but also recalled that he'd never promoted the idea that she could take time away from work without letting her feel guilty. In fact, he'd used her guilt.

"Thanks for offering me the job, Jeff, but I don't think I can help you. I've got my own clients to handle."

His face grew white, then mottled. "I'm afraid you don't have much choice."

She widened her eyes. "Why? What happens if I don't? Will you take away my partnership? Fire me?"

Jeff stood. "Don't push, Carolyn. I don't want to have to confront you on this. I'll win."

Swearing that she heard the click of a light going on in her head, Carolyn laughed. "No, Jeff. I win. I quit."

The words hung in the air; both of them seemed stunned by their impact.

"What?"

She tried them again, just to see if they felt as good the second time as they had the first. "I said, I quit." They felt better than good. They felt wonderful!

"You don't know what you're saying."

"Nothing ever felt this right," she said slowly, amazed by her reaction. For the first time in several years, Carolyn knew exactly what she wanted. Moreover, she was willing to go after it just as determinedly as she had gone after this job. Only now the goals were different.

The goals were Tony, a family, a small business, and most of all, love. Everything was mixed up, but it didn't matter. She wanted all of it.

"I'm leaving now." Jeff spoke slowly, stood and backed toward the door. "And I'm going to pretend that we didn't have this discussion. Later, when you've thought this through, you can see how silly the whole thing is. Until then we won't mention it again."

She felt lighter than air. "Thanks, but my decision stands."

"Don't be hasty." He reached the door. "I need another glass of champagne," he murmured uncertainly, then beat a hasty retreat, leaving her alone.

She smiled joyfully at her empty office. It was about time she grew up enough to recognize her own needs, her wishes, and face them. And Tony was a major part of those needs and wishes.

Reaching for the phone, she dialed the number she'd memorized but never used before.

When Tony answered, her heartbeat quickened just at the sound.

"I quit my job."

"Congratulations." His tone was wary.

If she wanted something badly enough, she had to go after it, Carolyn told herself. All he could say was no.... "Do you still want me to join you?"

"Always," he answered, his tone warning. "But only if I can have all of you. Not just the half that commutes back and forth to hard work."

"It's a deal." She laughed.

"Lady," Tony muttered huskily. "If you're on the level, you can't get here fast enough."

Carolyn grinned. "Don't I know it," she said softly. "And Tony? I don't have another job in the wings. I don't have anything. I might be broke in three or four months."

He didn't seem shocked. He didn't even seem surprised. In fact he laughed, long and hard. "No, you won't, lady," he said. "And, whatever you're thinking of taking from that office, don't. There isn't anything there that you'll ever need."

Carolyn looked around her, then grinned. "You're absolutely right. I'll be there directly."

"You're sure you know what you're doing? This isn't a whim, is it?"

"No whim." Confidence made her voice firm and sure. "You'd better find closet space for me in that ancient place. I think we're going into business together."

He laughed again. "In more ways than one, darlin'. It'll be a partnership of the rarest kind."

"I'll be right there," she promised again, not wanting him to be anywhere but in her arms. "I'm not even running to the house first."

"I'll be waiting. And Carolyn? I love you."

Love for him filled her heart and more, almost lifting her off the ground with its buoyancy. She finally said the words she'd been wanting to say all her life. "I love you, too."

"Damn, lady. You've made me one happy man," he said softly, the sound of his voice caressing her ear. "Hurry home, darlin'. I'm waiting for you."

A smile on her face to match the one in her heart, Carolyn slung her purse strap over her shoulder, glanced quickly around the office and said a silent goodbye. Without looking back, she walked out the door. Her step was jaunty, her smile bright and her mood lighter than it had been—oh, in a million years. It was time to pursue her dream.

Tony was waiting for her . . . Thank God!

$\mathcal{O}$nce upon a time...

There was the best romance series in all the land—Temptation

You loved the heroes of REBELS & ROGUES. Now discover the magic and fantasy of romance. *Pygmalion, Cinderella* and *Beauty and the Beast* have an enduring appeal—and are the inspiration for Temptation's exciting new yearlong miniseries, LOVERS & LEGENDS. Bestselling authors including Gina Wilkins, Glenda Sanders, JoAnn Ross and Tiffany White reweave these classic tales—with lots of sizzle! One book a month, LOVERS & LEGENDS continues in August 1993 with:

#453 THE PRINCE AND THE SHOWGIRL
JoAnn Ross
(Cinderella)

Live the fantasy...

LL8

HARLEQUIN®

Temptation

Take 4 bestselling love stories FREE

Plus get a FREE surprise gift!

Special Limited-time Offer

Mail to Harlequin Reader Service®

3010 Walden Avenue
P.O. Box 1867
Buffalo, N.Y. 14269-1867

YES! Please send me 4 free Harlequin Temptation® novels and my free surprise gift. Then send me 4 brand-new novels every month, which I will receive before they appear in bookstores. Bill me at the low price of $2.44 each plus 25¢ delivery and applicable sales tax, if any.* That's the complete price and—compared to the cover prices of $2.99 each—quite a bargain! I understand that accepting the books and gift places me under no obligation ever to buy any books. I can always return a shipment and cancel at any time. Even if I never buy another book from Harlequin, the 4 free books and the surprise gift are mine to keep forever.

142 BPA AJHR

Name _____ (PLEASE PRINT)

Address _____ Apt. No. _____

City _____ State _____ Zip _____

This offer is limited to one order per household and not valid to present Harlequin Temptation® subscribers.
*Terms and prices are subject to change without notice. Sales tax applicable in N.Y.

UTEMP-93R   ©1990 Harlequin Enterprises Limited

LIGHTS, CAMERA, ACTION!

Hollywood Dynasty

HARLEQUIN®
Temptation

The Kingstons are Hollywood—two generations of box-office legends in front of and behind the cameras. In this fast-paced world egos compete for the spotlight and intimate secrets make tabloid headlines. Gage—the cinematographer, Pierce—the actor and Claire—the producer struggle for success in an unpredictable business where a single film can make or break you.

By the time the credits roll, will they discover that the ultimate challenge is far more personal? Share the behind-the-scenes dreams and dramas in this blockbuster miniseries by Candace Schuler!

THE OTHER WOMAN, #451 (July 1993)
JUST ANOTHER PRETTY FACE, #459 (September 1993)
THE RIGHT DIRECTION, #467 (November 1993)

Coming soon to your favorite retail outlet.

Harlequin is proud to present our best authors and their best books. Always the best for your reading pleasure!

Throughout 1993, Harlequin will bring you exciting books by some of the top names in contemporary romance!

In July
look for
The Ties That Bind by

JAYNE ANN KRENTZ

Shannon wanted him seven days a week....

Dark, compelling, mysterious Garth Sheridan was no mere boy next door—even if he did rent the cottage beside Shannon Raine's.

She was intrigued by the hard-nosed exec, but for Shannon it was all or nothing. Either break the undeniable bonds between them... or tear down the barriers surrounding Garth and discover the truth.

Don't miss THE TIES THAT BIND ...
wherever Harlequin books are sold.

Fifty red-blooded, white-hot, true-blue hunks from every State in the Union!

Beginning in May, look for MEN MADE IN AMERICA! Written by some of our most popular authors, these stories feature fifty of the strongest, sexiest men, each from a different state in the union!

Two titles available every other month at your favorite retail outlet.

In July, look for:

CALL IT DESTINY by Jayne Ann Krentz (Arizona)
ANOTHER KIND OF LOVE by Mary Lynn Baxter (Arkansas)

In September, look for:

DECEPTIONS by Annette Broadrick (California)
STORMWALKER by Dallas Schulze (Colorado)

You won't be able to resist MEN MADE IN AMERICA!